CW00984061

Discoveries
Made Upon Men and
Matter and Some Poems

Ben Jonson

CONTENTS:

INTRODUCTION

Ben Jonson's "Discoveries" are, as he says in the few Latin words prefixed to them, "A wood—Sylva—of things and thoughts, in Greek "[Greek text]" [which has for its first meaning material, but is also applied peculiarly to kinds of wood, and to a wood], "from the multiplicity and variety of the material contained in it. For, as we are commonly used to call the infinite mixed multitude of growing trees a wood, so the ancients gave the name of Sylvae—Timber Trees—to books of theirs in which small works of various and diverse matter were promiscuously brought together. "

In this little book we have some of the best thoughts of one of the most vigorous minds that ever added to the strength of English literature. The songs added are a part of what Ben Jonson called his "Underwoods. "

Ben Jonson was of a north-country family from the Annan district that produced Thomas Carlyle. His father was ruined by religious persecution in the reign of Mary, became a preacher in Elizabeth's reign, and died a month before the poet's birth in 1573. Ben Jonson, therefore, was about nine years younger than Shakespeare, and he survived Shakespeare about twenty-one years, dying in August, 1637. Next to Shakespeare Ben Jonson was, in his own different way, the man of most mark in the story of the English drama. His mother, left poor, married again. Her second husband was a bricklayer, or small builder, and they lived for a time near Charing Cross in Hartshorn Lane. Ben Jonson was taught at the parish school of St. Martin's till he was discovered by William Camden, the historian. Camden was then second master in Westminster School. He procured for young Ben an admission into his school, and there laid firm foundations for that scholarship which the poet extended afterwards by private study until his learning grew to be sworn-brother to his wit.

Ben Jonson began the world poor. He worked for a very short time in his step-father's business. He volunteered to the wars in the Low Countries. He came home again, and joined the players. Before the end of Elizabeth's reign he had written three or four plays, in which he showed a young and ardent zeal for setting the world to rights, together with that high sense of the poet's calling which put lasting force into his work. He poured contempt on those who frittered life away. He urged on the poetasters and the mincing courtiers, who set their hearts on top-knots and affected movements of their lips and legs: -

> "That these vain joys in which their wills consume
> Such powers of wit and soul as are of force
> To raise their beings to eternity,
> May be converted on works fitting men;
> And for the practice of a forced look,
> An antic gesture, or a fustian phrase,
> Study the native frame of a true heart,
> An inward comeliness of bounty, knowledge,
> And spirit that may conform them actually
> To God's high figures, which they have in power. "

Ben Jonson's genius was producing its best work in the earlier years of the reign of James I. His Volpone, the Silent Woman, and the Alchemist first appeared side by side with some of the ripest works of Shakespeare in the years from 1605 to 1610. In the latter part of James's reign he produced masques for the Court, and turned with distaste from the public stage. When Charles I. became king, Ben Jonson was weakened in health by a paralytic stroke. He returned to the stage for a short time through necessity, but found his best friends in the best of the young poets of the day. These looked up to him as their father and their guide. Their own best efforts seemed best to them when they had won Ben Jonson's praise. They valued above all passing honours man could give the words, "My son, " in the old poet's greeting, which, as they said, "sealed them of the tribe of Ben. "

H. M.

SYLVA

Rerum et sententiarum quasi "[Greek text] dicta a multiplici materia et varietate in iis contenta. Quemadmodum enim vulgo solemus infinitam arborum nascentium indiscriminatim multitudinem Sylvam dicere: ita etiam libros suos in quibus variae et diversae materiae opuscula temere congesta erant, Sylvas appellabant antiqui: Timber-trees.

TIMBER;
OR, DISCOVERIES MADE UPON MEN AND MATTER,
AS THEY HAVE FLOWED OUT OF HIS DAILY READINGS,
OR HAD THEIR REFLUX TO HIS PECULIAR
NOTION OF THE TIMES.

Tecum habita, ut noris quam sit tibi curta supellex {11} PERS. Sat. 4.

Fortuna. —Ill fortune never crushed that man whom good fortune deceived not. I therefore have counselled my friends never to trust to her fairer side, though she seemed to make peace with them; but to place all things she gave them, so as she might ask them again without their trouble, she might take them from them, not pull them: to keep always a distance between her and themselves. He knows not his own strength that hath not met adversity. Heaven prepares good men with crosses; but no ill can happen to a good man. Contraries are not mixed. Yet that which happens to any man may to every man. But it is in his reason, what he accounts it and will make it.

Casus. —Change into extremity is very frequent and easy. As when a beggar suddenly grows rich, he commonly becomes a prodigal; for, to obscure his former obscurity, he puts on riot and excess.

Consilia. —No man is so foolish but may give another good counsel sometimes; and no man is so wise but may easily err, if he will take no others' counsel but his own. But very few men are wise by their own counsel, or learned by their own teaching. For he that was only taught by himself {12} had a fool to his master.

Fama. —A Fame that is wounded to the world would be better cured by another's apology than its own: for few can apply medicines well themselves. Besides, the man that is once hated, both his good and his evil deeds oppress him. He is not easily emergent.

Negotia. —In great affairs it is a work of difficulty to please all. And ofttimes we lose the occasions of carrying a business well and thoroughly by our too much haste. For passions are spiritual rebels, and raise sedition against the understanding.

Amor patriae. —There is a necessity all men should love their country: he that professeth the contrary may be delighted with his words, but his heart is there.

Ingenia. —Natures that are hardened to evil you shall sooner break than make straight; they are like poles that are crooked and dry, there is no attempting them.

Applausus. —We praise the things we hear with much more willingness than those we see, because we envy the present and reverence the past; thinking ourselves instructed by the one, and overlaid by the other.

Opinio. —Opinion is a light, vain, crude, and imperfect thing; settled in the imagination, but never arriving at the understanding, there to obtain the tincture of reason. We labour with it more than truth. There is much more holds us than presseth us. An ill fact is one thing, an ill fortune is another; yet both oftentimes sway us alike, by the error of our thinking.

Impostura. —Many men believe not themselves what they would persuade others; and less do the things which they would impose on others; but least of all know what they themselves most confidently boast. Only they set the sign of the cross over their outer doors, and sacrifice to their gut and their groin in their inner closets.

Jactura vitae. —What a deal of cold business doth a man misspend the better part of life in! in scattering compliments, tendering visits, gathering and venting news, following feasts and plays, making a little winter-love in a dark corner.

Hypocrita. —Puritanus Hypocrita est Haereticus, quem opinio propriae perspicaciae, qua sibi videtur, cum paucis in Ecclesia dogmatibus errores quosdam animadvertisse, de statu mentis deturbavit: unde sacro furore percitus, phrenetice pugnat contra magistratus, sic ratus obedientiam praestare Deo. {14}

Mutua auxilia. —Learning needs rest: sovereignty gives it. Sovereignty needs counsel: learning affords it. There is such a consociation of offices between the prince and whom his favour breeds, that they may help to sustain his power as he their knowledge. It is the greatest part of his liberality, his favour; and from whom doth he hear discipline more willingly, or the arts discoursed more gladly, than from those whom his own bounty and benefits have made able and faithful?

Cognit. univers. —In being able to counsel others, a man must be furnished with a universal store in himself, to the knowledge of all nature—that is, the matter and seed-plot: there are the seats of all argument and invention. But especially you must be cunning in the nature of man: there is the variety of things which are as the elements and letters, which his art and wisdom must rank and order to the present occasion. For we see not all letters in single words, nor all places in particular discourses. That cause seldom happens wherein a man will use all arguments.

Consiliarii adjunct. Probitas, Sapientia. —The two chief things that give a man reputation in counsel are the opinion of his honesty and the opinion of his wisdom: the authority of those two will persuade when the same counsels uttered by other persons less qualified are of no efficacy or working.

Vita recta. —Wisdom without honesty is mere craft and cozenage. And therefore the reputation of honesty must first be gotten, which cannot be but by living well. A good life is a main argument.

Obsequentia. —Humanitas. —Solicitudo. —Next a good life, to beget love in the persons we counsel, by dissembling our knowledge of ability in ourselves, and avoiding all suspicion of arrogance, ascribing all to their instruction, as an ambassador to his master, or a subject to his sovereign; seasoning all with humanity and sweetness, only expressing care and solicitude. And not to counsel rashly, or on the sudden, but with advice and meditation. (Dat nox consilium. {17a}) For many foolish things fall from wise men, if they speak in haste or be extemporal. It therefore behoves the giver of counsel to be circumspect; especially to beware of those with whom he is not thoroughly acquainted, lest any spice of rashness, folly, or self-love appear, which will be marked by new persons and men of experience in affairs.

Modestia. —Parrhesia. —And to the prince, or his superior, to behave himself modestly and with respect. Yet free from flattery or empire. Not with insolence or precept; but as the prince were already furnished with the parts he should have, especially in affairs of state. For in other things they will more easily suffer themselves to be taught or reprehended: they will not willingly contend, but hear, with Alexander, the answer the musician gave him: Absit, o rex, ut tu melius haec scias, quam ego. {17b}

Perspicuitas. —Elegantia. —A man should so deliver himself to the nature of the subject whereof he speaks, that his hearer may take knowledge of his discipline with some delight; and so apparel fair and good matter, that the studious of elegancy be not defrauded; redeem arts from their rough and braky seats, where they lay hid and overgrown with thorns, to a pure, open, and flowery light, where they may take the eye and be taken by the hand.

Natura non effaeta. —I cannot think Nature is so spent and decayed that she can bring forth nothing worth her former years. She is always the same, like herself; and when she collects her strength is abler still. Men are decayed, and studies: she is not.

Non nimium credendum antiquitati. —I know nothing can conduce more to letters than to examine the writings of the ancients, and not to rest in their sole authority, or take all upon trust from them, provided the plagues of judging and pronouncing against them be away; such as are envy, bitterness, precipitation, impudence, and scurrilous scoffing. For to all the observations of the ancients we have our own experience, which if we will use and apply, we have better means to pronounce. It is true they opened the gates, and made the way that went before us, but as guides, not commanders: Non domini nostri, sed duces fuere. {19a} Truth lies open to all; it is no man's several. Patet omnibus veritas; nondum est occupata. Multum ex illa, etiam futuris relicta est. {19b}

Dissentire licet, sed cum ratione. —If in some things I dissent from others, whose wit, industry, diligence, and judgment, I look up at and admire, let me not therefore hear presently of ingratitude and rashness. For I thank those that have taught me, and will ever; but yet dare not think the scope of their labour and inquiry was to envy their posterity what they also could add and find out.

Non mihi credendum sed veritati. —If I err, pardon me: Nulla ars simul et inventa est et absoluta. {19c} I do not desire to be equal to those that went before; but to have my reason examined with theirs, and so much faith to be given them, or me, as those shall evict. I am neither author nor fautor of any sect. I will have no man addict himself to me; but if I have anything right, defend it as Truth's, not mine, save as it conduceth to a common good. It profits not me to have any man fence or fight for me, to flourish, or take my side. Stand for truth, and 'tis enough.

Scientiae liberales. —Arts that respect the mind were ever reputed nobler than those that serve the body, though we less can be without them, as tillage, spinning, weaving, building, &c., without which we could scarce sustain life a day. But these were the works of every hand; the other of the brain only, and those the most generous and exalted wits and spirits, that cannot rest or acquiesce. The mind of man is still fed with labour: Opere pascitur.

Non vulgi sunt. —There is a more secret cause, and the power of liberal studies lies more hid than that it can be wrought out by profane wits. It is not every man's way to hit. There are men, I confess, that set the carat and value upon things as they love them; but science is not every man's mistress. It is as great a spite to be praised in the wrong place, and by a wrong person, as can be done to a noble nature.

Honesta ambitio. —If divers men seek fame or honour by divers ways, so both be honest, neither is to be blamed; but they that seek immortality are not only worthy of love, but of praise.

Maritus improbus. —He hath a delicate wife, a fair fortune, a family to go to and be welcome; yet he had rather be drunk with mine host and the fiddlers of such a town, than go home.

Afflictio pia magistra. —Affliction teacheth a wicked person some time to pray: prosperity never.

Deploratis facilis descensus Averni. —The devil take all. —Many might go to heaven with half the labour they go to hell, if they would venture their industry the right way; but "The devil take all! " quoth he that was choked in the mill-dam, with his four last words in his mouth.

AEgidius cursu superat. —A cripple in the way out-travels a footman or a post out of the way.

Prodigo nummi nauci. —Bags of money to a prodigal person are the same that cherry-stones are with some boys, and so thrown away.

Munda et sordida. —A woman, the more curious she is about her face is commonly the more careless about her house.

Debitum deploratum. —Of this spilt water there is a little to be gathered up: it is a desperate debt.

Latro sesquipedalis. —The thief {22} that had a longing at the gallows to commit one robbery more before he was hanged.

And like the German lord, when he went out of Newgate into the cart, took order to have his arms set up in his last herborough: said was he taken and committed upon suspicion of treason, no witness appearing against him; but the judges entertained him most civilly, discoursed with him, offered him the courtesy of the rack; but he confessed, &c.

Calumniae fructus. —I am beholden to calumny, that she hath so endeavoured and taken pains to belie me. It shall make me set a surer guard on myself, and keep a better watch upon my actions.

Impertinens. —A tedious person is one a man would leap a steeple from, gallop down any steep lull to avoid him; forsake his meat, sleep, nature itself, with all her benefits, to shun him. A mere impertinent; one that touched neither heaven nor earth in his discourse. He opened an entry into a fair room, but shut it again presently. I spoke to him of garlic, he answered asparagus; consulted him of marriage, he tells me of hanging, as if they went by one and the same destiny.

Bellum scribentium. —What a sight it is to see writers committed together by the ears for ceremonies, syllables, points, colons, commas, hyphens, and the like, fighting as for their fires and their altars; and angry that none are frighted at their noises and loud brayings under their asses' skins.

There is hope of getting a fortune without digging in these quarries. Sed meliore (in omne) ingenio animoque quam fortuna, sum usus. {23}

"Pingue solum lassat; sed juvat ipse labor. " {24a}

Differentia inter doctos et sciolos. —Wits made out their several expeditions then for the discovery of truth, to find out great and profitable knowledges; had their several instruments for the disquisition of arts. Now there are certain scioli or smatterers that are busy in the skirts and outsides of learning, and have scarce anything of solid literature to commend them. They may have some edging or trimming of a scholar, a welt or so; but it is no more.

Impostorum fucus. —Imposture is a specious thing, yet never worse than when it feigns to be best, and to none discovered sooner than the simplest. For truth and goodness are plain and open; but imposture is ever ashamed of the light.

Icunculorum motio. —A puppet-play must be shadowed and seen in the dark; for draw the curtain, et sordet gesticulatio. {24b}

Principes et administri. —There is a great difference in the understanding of some princes, as in the quality of their ministers about them. Some would dress their masters in gold, pearl, and all true jewels of majesty; others furnish them with feathers, bells, and ribands, and are therefore esteemed the fitter servants. But they are ever good men that must make good the times; if the men be naught, the times will be such. Finis exspectandus est in unoquoque hominum; animali ad mutationem promptissmo. {25a}

Scitum Hispanicum. —It is a quick saying with the Spaniards, Artes inter haeredes non dividi. {25b} Yet these have inherited their fathers' lying, and they brag of it. He is a narrow-minded man that affects a triumph in any glorious study; but to triumph in a lie, and a lie themselves have forged, is frontless. Folly often goes beyond her bounds; but Impudence knows none.

Non nova res livor. —Envy is no new thing, nor was it born only in our times. The ages past have brought it forth, and the coming ages will. So long as there are men fit for it, quorum odium virtute relicta placet, it will never be wanting. It is a barbarous envy, to take from those men's virtues which, because thou canst not arrive at, thou impotently despairest to imitate. Is it a crime in me that I know that which others had not yet known but from me? or that I am the author of many things which never would have come in thy thought but that I taught them? It is new but a foolish way you have found out, that whom you cannot equal or come near in doing, you would destroy or ruin with evil speaking; as if you had bound both your wits and natures 'prentices to slander, and then came forth the best artificers when you could form the foulest calumnies.

Nil gratius protervo lib. —Indeed nothing is of more credit or request now than a petulant paper, or scoffing verses; and it is but convenient to the times and manners we live with, to have then the worst writings and studies flourish when the best begin to be despised. Ill arts begin where good end.

Jam literae sordent. —*Pastus hodiern. ingen.* —The time was when men would learn and study good things, not envy those that had them. Then men were had in price for learning; now letters only make men vile. He is upbraidingly called a poet, as if it were a contemptible nick-name: but the professors, indeed, have made the learning cheap—railing and tinkling rhymers, whose writings the vulgar more greedily read, as being taken with the scurrility and petulancy of such wits. He shall not have a reader now unless he jeer and lie. It is the food of men's natures; the diet of the times; gallants cannot sleep else. The writer must lie and the gentle reader rests happy to hear the worthiest works misinterpreted, the clearest actions obscured, the innocentest life traduced: and in such a licence of lying, a field so fruitful of slanders, how can there be matter wanting to his laughter? Hence comes the epidemical infection; for how can they escape the contagion of the writings, whom the virulency of the calumnies hath not staved off from reading?

Sed seculi morbus. —Nothing doth more invite a greedy reader than an unlooked-for subject. And what more unlooked-for than to see a person of an unblamed life made ridiculous or odious by the artifice of lying? But it is the disease of the age; and no wonder if the world, growing old, begin to be infirm: old age itself is a disease. It is long since the sick world began to dote and talk idly: would she had but doted still! but her dotage is now broke forth into a madness, and become a mere frenzy.

Alastoris malitia. —This Alastor, who hath left nothing unsearched or unassailed by his impudent and licentious lying in his aguish writings (for he was in his cold quaking fit all the while), what hath he done more than a troublesome base cur? barked and made a noise afar off; had a fool or two to spit in his mouth, and cherish him with a musty bone? But they are rather enemies of my fame than me, these barkers.

Mali Choragi fuere. —It is an art to have so much judgment as to apparel a lie well, to give it a good dressing; that though the nakedness would show deformed and odious, the suiting of it might draw their readers. Some love any strumpet, be she never so shop-like or meretricious, in good clothes. But these, nature could not have formed them better to destroy their own testimony and overthrow their calumny.

Hear-say news. —That an elephant, in 1630, came hither ambassador from the Great Mogul, who could both write and read, and was every day allowed twelve cast of bread, twenty quarts of Canary sack, besides nuts and almonds the citizens' wives sent him. That he had a Spanish boy to his interpreter, and his chief negociation was to confer or practise with Archy, the principal fool of state, about stealing hence Windsor Castle and carrying it away on his back if he can.

Lingua sapientis, potius quam loquentis. —A wise tongue should not be licentious and wandering; but moved and, as it were, governed with certain reins from the heart and bottom of the breast: and it was excellently said of that philosopher, that there was a wall or parapet of teeth set in our mouth, to restrain the petulancy of our words; that the rashness of talking should not only be retarded by the guard and watch of our heart, but be fenced in and defended by certain strengths placed in the mouth itself, and within the lips. But you shall see some so abound with words, without any seasoning or taste of matter, in so profound a security, as while they are speaking, for the most part they confess to speak they know not what.

Of the two (if either were to be wished) I would rather have a plain downright wisdom, than a foolish and affected eloquence. For what is so furious and Bedlam like as a vain sound of chosen and excellent words, without any subject of sentence or science mixed?

Optanda. —Thersites Homeri. —Whom the disease of talking still once possesseth, he can never hold his peace. Nay, rather than he will not discourse he will hire men to hear him. And so heard, not hearkened unto, he comes off most times like a mountebank, that when he hath praised his medicines, finds none will take them, or trust him. He is like Homer's Thersites.

[Greek text]; speaking without judgement or measure.

> "Loquax magis, quam facundus,
> Satis loquentiae, sapientiae parum. {31a}
> [Greek verse]. {31b}

> Optimus est homini linguae thesaurus, et ingens
> Gratia, quae parcis mensurat singula verbis. "

Homeri Ulysses. —Demacatus Plutarchi. —Ulysses, in Homer, is made a long-thinking man before he speaks; and Epaminondas is celebrated by Pindar to be a man that, though he knew much, yet he spoke but little. Demacatus, when on the bench he was long silent and said nothing, one asking him if it were folly in him, or want of language, he answered, "A fool could never hold his peace. " {31c} For too much talking is ever the index of a fool.

> "Dum tacet indoctus, poterit cordatus haberi;
> Is morbos animi namque tacendo tegit. " {32a}

Nor is that worthy speech of Zeno the philosopher to be passed over with the note of ignorance; who being invited to a feast in Athens, where a great prince's ambassadors were entertained, and was the only person that said nothing at the table; one of them with courtesy asked him, "What shall we return from thee, Zeno, to the prince our master, if he asks us of thee? " "Nothing, " he replied, "more but that you found an old man in Athens that knew to be silent amongst his cups. " It was near a miracle to see an old man silent, since talking is the disease of age; but amongst cups makes it fully a wonder.

Argute dictum. —It was wittily said upon one that was taken for a great and grave man so long as he held his peace, "This man might have been a counsellor of state, till he spoke; but having spoken, not the beadle of the ward. " [Greek text]. {32b} Pytag. quam laudabilis! [Greek text]. Linguam cohibe, prae aliis omnibus, ad deorum exemplum. {33a} Digito compesce labellum. {33b}

Acutius cernuntur vitia quam virtutes. —There is almost no man but he sees clearlier and sharper the vices in a speaker, than the virtues. And there are many, that with more ease will find fault with what is spoken foolishly than can give allowance to that wherein you are wise silently. The treasure of a fool is always in his tongue, said the witty comic poet; {33c} and it appears not in anything more than in that nation, whereof one, when he had got the inheritance of an unlucky old grange, would needs sell it; {33d} and to draw buyers proclaimed the virtues of it. Nothing ever thrived on it, saith he. No owner of it ever died in his bed; some hung, some drowned themselves; some were banished, some starved; the trees were all blasted; the swine died of the measles, the cattle of the murrain, the sheep of the rot; they that stood were ragged, bare, and bald as your hand; nothing was ever reared there, not a duckling, or a goose. Hospitium fuerat calamitatis. {34a} Was not this man like to sell it?

Vulgi expectatio. —Expectation of the vulgar is more drawn and held with newness than goodness; we see it in fencers, in players, in poets, in preachers, in all where fame promiseth anything; so it be new, though never so naught and depraved, they run to it, and are taken. Which shews, that the only decay or hurt of the best men's reputation with the people is, their wits have out-lived the people's palates. They have been too much or too long a feast.

Claritas patriae. —Greatness of name in the father oft-times helps not forth, but overwhelms the son; they stand too near one another. The shadow kills the growth: so much, that we see the grandchild come more and oftener to be heir of the first, than doth the second: he dies between; the possession is the third's.

Eloquentia. —Eloquence is a great and diverse thing: nor did she yet ever favour any man so much as to become wholly his. He is happy that can arrive to any degree of her grace. Yet there are who prove themselves masters of her, and absolute lords; but I believe they may mistake their evidence: for it is one thing to be eloquent in the schools, or in the hall; another at the bar, or in the pulpit. There is a difference between mooting and pleading; between fencing and fighting. To make arguments in my study, and confute them, is easy; where I answer myself, not an adversary. So I can see whole volumes dispatched by the umbratical doctors on all sides: but draw these forth into the just lists: let them appear sub dio, and they are changed with the place, like bodies bred in the shade; they cannot suffer the sun or a shower, nor bear the open air; they scarce can find themselves, that they were wont to domineer so among their auditors: but indeed I would no more choose a rhetorician for reigning in a school, than I would a pilot for rowing in a pond.

Amor et odium. —Love that is ignorant, and hatred, have almost the same ends: many foolish lovers wish the same to their friends, which their enemies would: as to wish a friend banished, that they might accompany him in exile; or some great want, that they might relieve him; or a disease, that they might sit by him. They make a causeway to their country by injury, as if it were not honester to do nothing than to seek a way to do good by a mischief.

Injuria. —Injuries do not extinguish courtesies: they only suffer them not to appear fair. For a man that doth me an injury after a courtesy, takes not away that courtesy, but defaces it: as he that writes other verses upon my verses, takes not away the first letters, but hides them.

Beneficia. —Nothing is a courtesy unless it be meant us; and that friendly and lovingly. We owe no thanks to rivers, that they carry our boats; or winds, that they be favouring and fill our sails; or meats, that they be nourishing. For these are what they are necessarily. Horses carry us, trees shade us, but they know it not. It is true, some men may receive a courtesy and not know it; but never any man received it from him that knew it not. Many men have been cured of diseases by accidents; but they were not remedies. I myself have known one helped of an ague by falling into a water; another whipped out of a fever; but no man would ever use these for medicines. It is the mind, and not the event, that distinguisheth the courtesy from wrong. My adversary may offend the judge with his pride and impertinences, and I win my cause; but he meant it not to me as a courtesy. I scaped pirates by being shipwrecked; was the wreck a benefit therefore? No; the doing of courtesies aright is the mixing of the respects for his own sake and for mine. He that doeth them merely for his own sake is like one that feeds his cattle to sell them; he hath his horse well dressed for Smithfield.

Valor rerum. —The price of many things is far above what they are bought and sold for. Life and health, which are both inestimable, we have of the physician; as learning and knowledge, the true tillage of the mind, from our schoolmasters. But the fees of the one or the salary of the other never answer the value of what we received, but served to gratify their labours.

Memoria. —Memory, of all the powers of the mind, is the most delicate and frail; it is the first of our faculties that age invades. Seneca, the father, the rhetorician, confesseth of himself he had a miraculous one, not only to receive but to hold. I myself could, in my youth, have repeated all that ever I had made, and so continued till I was past forty; since, it is much decayed in me. Yet I can repeat whole books that I have read, and poems of some selected friends which I have liked to charge my memory with. It was wont to be faithful to me; but shaken with age now, and sloth, which weakens the strongest abilities, it may perform somewhat, but cannot promise much. By exercise it is to be made better and serviceable. Whatsoever

I pawned with it while I was young and a boy, it offers me readily, and without stops; but what I trust to it now, or have done of later years, it lays up more negligently, and oftentimes loses; so that I receive mine own (though frequently called for) as if it were new and borrowed. Nor do I always find presently from it what I seek; but while I am doing another thing, that I laboured for will come; and what I sought with trouble will offer itself when I am quiet. Now, in some men I have found it as happy as Nature, who, whatsoever they read or pen, they can say without book presently, as if they did then write in their mind. And it is more a wonder in such as have a swift style, for their memories are commonly slowest; such as torture their writings, and go into council for every word, must needs fix somewhat, and make it their own at last, though but through their own vexation.

Comit. suffragia. —Suffrages in Parliament are numbered, not weighed; nor can it be otherwise in those public councils where nothing is so unequal as the equality; for there, how odd soever men's brains or wisdoms are, their power is always even and the same.

Stare a partibus. —Some actions, be they never so beautiful and generous, are often obscured by base and vile misconstructions, either out of envy or ill-nature, that judgeth of others as of itself. Nay, the times are so wholly grown to be either partial or malicious, that if he be a friend all sits well about him, his very vices shall be virtues; if an enemy, or of the contrary faction, nothing is good or tolerable in him; insomuch that we care not to discredit and shame our judgments to soothe our passions.

Deus in creaturis. —Man is read in his face; God in His creatures; not as the philosopher, the creature of glory, reads him; but as the divine, the servant of humility; yet even he must take care not to be too curious. For to utter truth of God but as he thinks only, may be dangerous, who is best known by our not knowing. Some things of Him, so much as He hath revealed or commanded, it is not only lawful but necessary for us to know; for therein our ignorance was the first cause of our wickedness.

Veritas proprium hominis. —Truth is man's proper good, and the only immortal thing was given to our mortality to use. No good Christian or ethnic, if he be honest, can miss it; no statesman or patriot should. For without truth all the actions of mankind are craft, malice, or what you will, rather than wisdom. Homer says he hates him worse than hell-mouth that utters one thing with his tongue and keeps another in his breast. Which high expression was grounded on divine reason; for a lying mouth is a stinking pit, and murders with the contagion it venteth. Beside, nothing is lasting that is feigned; it will have another face than it had, ere long. {41} As Euripides saith, "No lie ever grows old. "

Nullum vitium sine patrocinio. —It is strange there should be no vice without its patronage, that when we have no other excuse we will say, we love it, we cannot forsake it. As if that made it not more a fault. We cannot, because we think we cannot, and we love it because we will defend it. We will rather excuse it than be rid of it. That we cannot is pretended; but that we will not is the true reason. How many have I known that would not have their vices hid? nay, and, to be noted, live like Antipodes to others in the same city? never see the sun rise or set in so many years, but be as they were watching a corpse by torch-light; would not sin the common way, but held that a kind of rusticity; they would do it new, or contrary, for the infamy; they were ambitious of living backward; and at last arrived at that, as they would love nothing but the vices, not the vicious customs. It was impossible to reform these natures; they were dried and hardened in their ill. They may say they desired to leave it, but do not trust them; and they may think they desire it, but they may lie for all that; they are a little angry with their follies now and then; marry, they come into grace with them again quickly. They will confess they are offended with their manner of living like enough; who is not? When they can put me in security that they are more than offended, that they hate it, then I will hearken to them, and perhaps believe them; but many now- a-days love and hate their ill together.

De vere argutis. —I do hear them say often some men are not witty, because they are not everywhere witty; than which nothing is more foolish. If an eye or a nose be an excellent part in the face, therefore be all eye or nose! I think the eyebrow, the forehead, the cheek, chin, lip, or any part else are as necessary and natural in the place. But now nothing is good that is natural; right and natural language seems to have least of the wit in it; that which is writhed and tortured is counted the more exquisite. Cloth of bodkin or tissue must be embroidered; as if no face were fair that were not powdered or painted! no beauty to be had but in wresting and writhing our own tongue! Nothing is fashionable till it be deformed; and this is to write like a gentleman. All must be affected and preposterous as our gallants' clothes, sweet-bags, and night-dressings, in which you would think our men lay in, like ladies, it is so curious.

Censura de poetis. —Nothing in our age, I have observed, is more preposterous than the running judgments upon poetry and poets; when we shall hear those things commended and cried up for the best writings which a man would scarce vouchsafe to wrap any wholesome drug in; he would never light his tobacco with them. And those men almost named for miracles, who yet are so vile that if a man should go about to examine and correct them, he must make all they have done but one blot. Their good is so entangled with their bad as forcibly one must draw on the other's death with it. A sponge dipped in ink will do all: -

> "—Comitetur Punica librum
> Spongia. —" {44a}

Et paulo post,

> "Non possunt . .. multae . .. liturae
> . .. una litura potest. "

Cestius—Cicero—Heath—Taylor—Spenser. —Yet their vices have not hurt them; nay, a great many they have profited, for they have been loved for nothing else. And this false opinion grows strong against the best men, if once it take root with the ignorant. Cestius, in his time, was preferred to Cicero, so far as the ignorant durst. They learned him without book, and had him often in their mouths; but a man cannot imagine that thing so foolish or rude but will find and enjoy an admirer; at least a reader or spectator. The puppets are seen now in despite of the players; Heath's epigrams and the Sculler's poems have their applause. There are never wanting that dare prefer the worst preachers, the worst pleaders, the worst poets; not that the better have left to write or speak better, but that they that hear them judge worse; Non illi pejus dicunt, sed hi corruptius judicant. Nay, if it were put to the question of the water-rhymer's works, against Spenser's, I doubt not but they would find more suffrages; because the most favour common vices, out of a prerogative the vulgar have to lose their judgments and like that which is naught.

Poetry, in this latter age, hath proved but a mean mistress to such as have wholly addicted themselves to her, or given their names up to her family. They who have but saluted her on the by, and now and then tendered their visits, she hath done much for, and advanced in the way of their own professions (both the law and the gospel) beyond all they could have hoped or done for themselves without her favour. Wherein she doth emulate the judicious but preposterous bounty of the time's grandees, who accumulate all they can upon the parasite or fresh-man in their friendship; but think an old client or honest servant bound by his place to write and starve.

Indeed, the multitude commend writers as they do fencers or wrestlers, who if they come in robustiously and put for it with a deal of violence are received for the braver fellows; when many times their own rudeness is a cause of their disgrace, and a slight touch of their adversary gives all that boisterous force the foil. But in these things the unskilful are naturally deceived, and judging wholly by the bulk, think rude things greater than polished, and scattered more numerous than composed; nor think this only to be true in the sordid multitude, but the neater sort of our gallants; for all are the multitude, only they differ in clothes, not in judgment or understanding.

De Shakspeare nostrat. —Augustus in Hat. —I remember the players have often mentioned it as an honour to Shakspeare, that in his writing (whatsoever he penned) he never blotted out a line. My answer hath been, "Would he had blotted a thousand, " which they thought a malevolent speech. I had not told posterity this but for their ignorance who chose that circumstance to commend their friend by wherein he most faulted; and to justify mine own candour, for I loved the man, and do honour his memory on this side idolatry as much as any. He was, indeed, honest, and of an open and free nature, had an excellent phantasy, brave notions, and gentle expressions, wherein he flowed with that facility that sometimes it was necessary he should be stopped. "Sufflaminandus erat, " {47a} as Augustus said of Haterius. His wit was in his own power; would the rule of it had been so, too. Many times he fell into those things, could not escape laughter, as when he said in the person of Caesar, one speaking to him, "Caesar, thou dost me wrong. " He replied, "Caesar did never wrong but with just cause; " and such like, which were ridiculous. But he redeemed his vices with his virtues. There was ever more in him to be praised than to be pardoned.

Ingeniorum discrimina. —Not. 1. —In the difference of wits I have observed there are many notes; and it is a little maistry to know them, to discern what every nature, every disposition will bear; for before we sow our land we should plough it. There are no fewer forms of minds than of bodies amongst us. The variety is incredible, and therefore we must search. Some are fit to make divines, some poets, some lawyers, some physicians; some to be sent to the plough, and trades.

There is no doctrine will do good where nature is wanting. Some wits are swelling and high; others low and still; some hot and fiery; others cold and dull; one must have a bridle, the other a spur.

Not. 2. —There be some that are forward and bold; and these will do every little thing easily. I mean that is hard by and next them, which they will utter unretarded without any shamefastness. These never perform much, but quickly. They are what they are on the sudden; they show presently, like grain that, scattered on the top of the ground, shoots up, but takes no root; has a yellow blade, but the ear empty. They are wits of good promise at first, but there is an ingenistitium; {49a} they stand still at sixteen, they get no higher.

Not. 3. —You have others that labour only to ostentation; and are ever more busy about the colours and surface of a work than in the matter and foundation, for that is hid, the other is seen.

Not. 4. —Others that in composition are nothing but what is rough and broken. Quae per salebras, altaque saxa cadunt. {49b} And if it would come gently, they trouble it of purpose. They would not have it run without rubs, as if that style were more strong and manly that struck the ear with a kind of unevenness. These men err not by chance, but knowingly and willingly; they are like men that affect a fashion by themselves; have some singularity in a ruff cloak, or hat-band; or their beards specially cut to provoke beholders, and set a mark upon themselves. They would be reprehended while they are looked on. And this vice, one that is authority with the rest, loving, delivers over to them to be imitated; so that ofttimes the faults which be fell into the others seek for. This is the danger, when vice becomes a precedent.

Not. 5. —Others there are that have no composition at all; but a kind of tuning and rhyming fall in what they write. It runs and slides, and only makes a sound. Women's poets they are called, as you have women's tailors.

"They write a verse as smooth, as soft as cream, In which there is no torrent, nor scarce stream. "

You may sound these wits and find the depth of them with your middle finger. They are cream-bowl or but puddle-deep.

Not. 6. —Some that turn over all books, and are equally searching in all papers; that write out of what they presently find or meet, without choice. By which means it happens that what they have discredited and impugned in one week, they have before or after extolled the same in another. Such are all the essayists, even their master Montaigne. These, in all they write, confess still what books they have read last, and therein their own folly so much, that they bring it to the stake raw and undigested; not that the place did need it neither, but that they thought themselves furnished and would vent it

Not. 7. —Some, again who, after they have got authority, or, which is less, opinion, by their writings, to have read much, dare presently to feign whole books and authors, and lie safely. For what never was, will not easily be found, not by the most curious.

Not. 8. —And some, by a cunning protestation against all reading, and false vendition of their own naturals, think to divert the sagacity of their readers from themselves, and cool the scent of their own fox-like thefts; when yet they are so rank, as a man may find whole pages together usurped from one author; their necessities compelling them to read for present use, which could not be in many books; and so come forth more ridiculously and palpably guilty than those who, because they cannot trace, they yet would slander their industry.

Not. 9. —But the wretcheder are the obstinate contemners of all helps and arts; such as presuming on their own naturals (which, perhaps, are excellent), dare deride all diligence, and seem to mock at the terms when they understand not the things; thinking that way to get off wittily with their ignorance. These are imitated often by such as are their peers in negligence, though they cannot be in nature; and they utter all they can think with a kind of violence and indisposition, unexamined, without relation either to person, place, or any fitness else; and the more wilful and stubborn they are in it the more learned they are esteemed of the multitude, through their excellent vice of judgment, who think those things the stronger that have no art; as if to break were better than to open, or to rend asunder gentler than to loose.

Not. 10. —It cannot but come to pass that these men who commonly seek to do more than enough may sometimes happen on something that is good and great; but very seldom: and when it comes it doth not recompense the rest of their ill. For their jests, and their sentences (which they only and ambitiously seek for) stick out, and are more eminent, because all is sordid and vile about them; as lights are more discerned in a thick darkness than a faint shadow. Now, because they speak all they can (however unfitly), they are thought to have the greater copy; where the learned use ever election and a mean, they look back to what they intended at first, and make all an even and proportioned body. The true artificer will not run away from Nature as he were afraid of her, or depart from life and the likeness of truth, but speak to the capacity of his hearers. And though his language differ from the vulgar somewhat, it shall not fly from all humanity, with the Tamerlanes and Tamer- chains of the late age, which had nothing in them but the scenical strutting and furious vociferation to warrant them to the ignorant gapers. He knows it is his only art so to carry it, as none but artificers perceive it. In the meantime, perhaps, he is called barren, dull, lean, a poor writer, or by what contumelious word can come in their cheeks, by these men who, without labour, judgment, knowledge, or almost sense, are received or preferred before him. He gratulates them and their fortune. Another age, or juster men, will acknowledge the virtues of his studies, his wisdom in dividing, his subtlety in arguing, with what strength he doth inspire his readers, with what sweetness he strokes them; in inveighing, what sharpness; in jest, what urbanity he uses; how he doth reign in men's affections; how invade and break in upon them, and makes their minds like the thing he writes. Then in his elocution to behold what word is proper, which hath ornaments, which height, what is beautifully translated, where figures are fit, which gentle, which strong, to show the composition manly; and how he hath avoided faint, obscure, obscene, sordid, humble, improper, or effeminate phrase; which is not only praised of the most, but commended (which is worse), especially for that it is naught.

Ignorantia animae. —I know no disease of the soul but ignorance, not of the arts and sciences, but of itself; yet relating to those it is a pernicious evil, the darkener of man's life, the disturber of his reason, and common confounder of truth, with which a man goes groping in the dark, no otherwise than if he were blind. Great understandings are most racked and troubled with it; nay, sometimes they will rather choose to die than not to know the things they study for. Think, then, what an evil it is, and what good the contrary.

Scientia. —Knowledge is the action of the soul and is perfect without the senses, as having the seeds of all science and virtue in itself; but not without the service of the senses; by these organs the soul works: she is a perpetual agent, prompt and subtle; but often flexible and erring, entangling herself like a silkworm, but her reason is a weapon with two edges, and cuts through. In her indagations oft-times new scents put her by, and she takes in errors into her by the same conduits she doth truths.

Otium Studiorum. —Ease and relaxation are profitable to all studies. The mind is like a bow, the stronger by being unbent. But the temper in spirits is all, when to command a man's wit, when to favour it. I have known a man vehement on both sides, that knew no mean, either to intermit his studies or call upon them again. When he hath set himself to writing he would join night to day, press upon himself without release, not minding it, till he fainted; and when he left off, resolve himself into all sports and looseness again, that it was almost a despair to draw him to his book; but once got to it, he grew stronger and more earnest by the ease. His whole powers were renewed; he would work out of himself what he desired, but with such excess as his study could not be ruled; he knew not how to dispose his own abilities, or husband them; he was of that immoderate power against himself. Nor was he only a strong, but an absolute speaker and writer; but his subtlety did not show itself; his judgment thought that a vice; for the ambush hurts more that is hid. He never forced his language, nor went out of the highway of speaking but for some great necessity or apparent profit; for he denied figures to be invented for ornament, but for aid; and still thought it an extreme madness to bind or wrest that which ought to be right.

Stili eminentia. —Virgil. —Tully. —Sallust. —It is no wonder men's eminence appears but in their own way. Virgil's felicity left him in prose, as Tully's forsook him in verse. Sallust's orations are read in the honour of story, yet the most eloquent. Plato's speech, which he made for Socrates, is neither worthy of the patron nor the person defended. Nay, in the same kind of oratory, and where the matter is one, you shall have him that reasons strongly, open negligently; another that prepares well, not fit so well. And this happens not only to brains, but to bodies. One can wrestle well, another run well, a third leap or throw the bar, a fourth lift or stop a cart going; each hath his way of strength. So in other creatures—some dogs are for the deer, some for the wild boar, some are fox-hounds, some otter-hounds. Nor are all horses for the coach or saddle, some are for the cart and paniers.

De Claris Oratoribus. —I have known many excellent men that would speak suddenly to the admiration of their hearers, who upon study and premeditation have been forsaken by their own wits, and no way answered their fame; their eloquence was greater than their reading, and the things they uttered better than those they knew; their fortune deserved better of them than their care. For men of present spirits, and of greater wits than study, do please more in the things they invent than in those they bring. And I have heard some of them compelled to speak, out of necessity, that have so infinitely exceeded themselves, as it was better both for them and their auditory that they were so surprised, not prepared. Nor was it safe then to cross them, for their adversary, their anger made them more eloquent. Yet these men I could not but love and admire, that they returned to their studies. They left not diligence (as many do) when their rashness prospered; for diligence is a great aid, even to an indifferent wit; when we are not contented with the examples of our own age, but would know the face of the former. Indeed, the more we confer with the more we profit by, if the persons be chosen.

Dominus Verulamius. —One, though he be excellent and the chief, is not to be imitated alone; for no imitator ever grew up to his author; likeness is always on this side truth. Yet there happened in my time one noble speaker who was full of gravity in his speaking; his language (where he could spare or pass by a jest) was nobly censorious. No man ever spake more neatly, more pressly, more weightily, or suffered less emptiness, less idleness, in what he uttered. No member of his speech but consisted of his own graces. His hearers could not cough, or look aside from him, without loss. He commanded where he spoke, and had his judges angry and pleased at his devotion. No man had their affections more in his power. The fear of every man that heard him was lest he should make an end.

Scriptorum catalogus. {59a} Cicero is said to be the only wit that the people of Rome had equalled to their empire. Ingenium par imperio. We have had many, and in their several ages (to take in but the former seculum) Sir Thomas More, the elder Wiat, Henry Earl of Surrey, Chaloner, Smith, Eliot, B. Gardiner, were for their times admirable; and the more, because they began eloquence with us. Sir Nicolas Bacon was singular, and almost alone, in the beginning of Queen Elizabeth's time. Sir Philip Sidney and Mr. Hooker (in different matter) grew great masters of wit and language, and in whom all vigour of invention and strength of judgment met. The Earl of Essex, noble and high; and Sir Walter Raleigh, not to be contemned, either for judgment or style. Sir Henry Savile, grave, and truly lettered; Sir Edwin Sandys, excellent in both; Lord Egerton, the Chancellor, a grave and great orator, and best when he was provoked; but his learned and able (though unfortunate) successor is he who hath filled up all numbers, and performed that in our tongue which may be compared or preferred either to insolent Greece or haughty Rome. In short, within his view, and about his times, were all the wits born that could honour a language or help study. Now things daily fall, wits grow downward, and eloquence grows backward; so that he may be named and stand as the mark and [Greek text] of our language.

De augmentis scientiarum. —Julius Caesar. —Lord St. Alban. —I have ever observed it to have been the office of a wise patriot, among the greatest affairs of the State, to take care of the commonwealth of learning. For schools, they are the seminaries of State; and nothing is worthier the study of a statesman than that part of the republic which we call the advancement of letters. Witness the care of Julius Caesar, who, in the heat of the civil war, writ his books of Analogy, and dedicated them to Tully. This made the late Lord St. Alban entitle his work Novum Organum; which, though by the most of superficial men, who cannot get beyond the title of nominals, it is not penetrated nor understood, it really openeth all defects of learning whatsoever, and is a book

"Qui longum note scriptori proroget aevum. " {62a}

My conceit of his person was never increased toward him by his place or honours; but I have and do reverence him for the greatness that was only proper to himself, in that he seemed to me ever, by his work, one of the greatest men, and most worthy of admiration, that had been in many ages. In his adversity I ever prayed that God would give him strength; for greatness he could not want. Neither could I condole in a word or syllable for him, as knowing no accident could do harm to virtue, but rather help to make it manifest.

De corruptela morum. —There cannot be one colour of the mind, another of the wit. If the mind be staid, grave, and composed, the wit is so; that vitiated, the other is blown and deflowered. Do we not see, if the mind languish, the members are dull? Look upon an effeminate person, his very gait confesseth him. If a man be fiery, his motion is so; if angry, it is troubled and violent. So that we may conclude wheresoever manners and fashions are corrupted, language is. It imitates the public riot. The excess of feasts and apparel are the notes of a sick state, and the wantonness of language of a sick mind.

De rebus mundanis. —If we would consider what our affairs are indeed, not what they are called, we should find more evils belonging to us than happen to us. How often doth that which was called a calamity prove the beginning and cause of a man's happiness? and, on the contrary, that which happened or came to another with great gratulation and applause, how it hath lifted him but a step higher to his ruin? as if he stood before where he might fall safely.

Vulgi mores. —Morbus comitialis. —The vulgar are commonly ill-natured, and always grudging against their governors: which makes that a prince has more business and trouble with them than ever Hercules had with the bull or any other beast; by how much they have more heads than will be reined with one bridle. There was not that variety of beasts in the ark, as is of beastly natures in the multitude; especially when they come to that iniquity to censure their sovereign's actions. Then all the counsels are made good or bad by the events; and it falleth out that the same facts receive from them the names, now of diligence, now of vanity, now of majesty, now of fury; where they ought wholly to hang on his mouth, as he to consist of himself, and not others' counsels.

Princeps. —After God, nothing is to be loved of man like the prince; he violates Nature that doth it not with his whole heart. For when he hath put on the care of the public good and common safety, I am a wretch, and put off man, if I do not reverence and honour him, in whose charge all things divine and human are placed. Do but ask of Nature why all living creatures are less delighted with meat and drink that sustains them than with venery that wastes them? and she will tell thee, the first respects but a private, the other a common good, propagation.

De eodem. —Orpheus' Hymn. —He is the arbiter of life and death: when he finds no other subject for his mercy, he should spare himself. All his punishments are rather to correct than to destroy. Why are prayers with Orpheus said to be the daughters of Jupiter, but that princes are thereby admonished that the petitions of the wretched ought to have more weight with them than the laws themselves.

De opt. Rege Jacobo. —It was a great accumulation to His Majesty's deserved praise that men might openly visit and pity those whom his greatest prisons had at any time received or his laws condemned.

De Princ. adjunctis. —Sed vere prudens haud concipi possit Princeps, nisi simul et bonus. —Lycurgus. —Sylla. —Lysander. —Cyrus. —Wise is rather the attribute of a prince than learned or good. The learned man profits others rather than himself; the good man rather himself than others; but the prince commands others, and doth himself.

The wise Lycurgus gave no law but what himself kept. Sylla and Lysander did not so; the one living extremely dissolute himself, enforced frugality by the laws; the other permitted those licenses to others which himself abstained from. But the prince's prudence is his chief art and safety. In his counsels and deliberations he foresees the future times: in the equity of his judgment he hath remembrance of the past, and knowledge of what is to be done or avoided for the present. Hence the Persians gave out their Cyrus to have been nursed by a bitch, a creature to encounter it, as of sagacity to seek out good; showing that wisdom may accompany fortitude, or it leaves to be, and puts on the name of rashness.

De malign. studentium. —There be some men are born only to suck out the poison of books: Habent venenum pro victu; imo, pro deliciis. {66a} And such are they that only relish the obscene and foul things in poets, which makes the profession taxed. But by whom? Men that watch for it; and, had they not had this hint, are so unjust valuers of letters as they think no learning good but what brings in gain. It shows they themselves would never have been of the professions they are but for the profits and fees. But if another learning, well used, can instruct to good life, inform manners, no less persuade and lead men than they threaten and compel, and have no reward, is it therefore the worst study? I could never think the study of wisdom confined only to the philosopher, or of piety to the divine, or of state to the politic; but that he which can feign a commonwealth (which is the poet) can govern it with counsels, strengthen it with laws, correct it with judgments, inform it with religion and morals, is all these. We do not require in him mere elocution, or an excellent faculty in verse, but the exact knowledge of all virtues and their contraries, with ability to render the one loved, the other hated, by his proper embattling them. The philosophers did insolently, to challenge only to themselves that which the greatest generals and gravest counsellors never durst. For such had rather do than promise the best things.

Controvers. scriptores. —More Andabatarum qui clausis oculis pugnant. —Some controverters in divinity are like swaggerers in a tavern that catch that which stands next them, the candlestick or pots; turn everything into a weapon: ofttimes they fight blindfold, and both beat the air. The one milks a he-goat, the other holds under a sieve. Their arguments are as fluxive as liquor spilt upon a table, which with your finger you may drain as you will. Such controversies or disputations (carried with more labour than profit) are odious; where most times the truth is lost in the midst or left untouched. And the fruit of their fight is, that they spit one upon another, and are both defiled. These fencers in religion I like not.

Morbi. —The body hath certain diseases that are with less evil tolerated than removed. As if to cure a leprosy a man should bathe himself with the warm blood of a murdered child, so in the Church some errors may be dissimuled with less inconvenience than they can be discovered.

Jactantia intempestiva. —Men that talk of their own benefits are not believed to talk of them because they have done them; but to have done them because they might talk of them. That which had been great, if another had reported it of them, vanisheth, and is nothing, if he that did it speak of it. For men, when they cannot destroy the deed, will yet be glad to take advantage of the boasting, and lessen it.

Adulatio. —I have seen that poverty makes me do unfit things; but honest men should not do them; they should gain otherwise. Though a man be hungry, he should not play the parasite. That hour wherein I would repent me to be honest, there were ways enough open for me to be rich. But flattery is a fine pick-lock of tender ears; especially of those whom fortune hath borne high upon their wings, that submit their dignity and authority to it, by a soothing of themselves. For, indeed, men could never be taken in that abundance with the springes of others' flattery, if they began not there; if they did but remember how much more profitable the bitterness of truth were, than all the honey distilling from a whorish voice, which is not praise, but poison. But now it is come to that extreme folly, or rather madness, with some, that he that flatters them modestly or sparingly is thought to malign them. If their friend consent not to their vices, though he do not contradict them, he is nevertheless an enemy. When they do all things the worst way, even then they look for praise. Nay, they will hire fellows to flatter them with suits and suppers, and to prostitute their judgments. They have livery-friends, friends of the dish, and of the spit, that wait their turns, as my lord has his feasts and guests.

De vita humana. —I have considered our whole life is like a play: wherein every man forgetful of himself, is in travail with expression of another. Nay, we so insist in imitating others, as we cannot when it is necessary return to ourselves; like children, that imitate the vices of stammerers so long, till at last they become such; and make the habit to another nature, as it is never forgotten.

De piis et probis. —Good men are the stars, the planets of the ages wherein they live and illustrate the times. God did never let them be wanting to the world: as Abel, for an example of innocency, Enoch of purity, Noah of trust in God's mercies, Abraham of faith, and so of the rest. These, sensual men thought mad because they would not be partakers or practisers of their madness. But they, placed high on the top of all virtue, looked down on the stage of the world and contemned the play of fortune. For though the most be players, some must be spectators.

Mores aulici. —I have discovered that a feigned familiarity in great ones is a note of certain usurpation on the less. For great and popular men feign themselves to be servants to others to make those slaves to them. So the fisher provides bait for the trout, roach, dace, &c., that they may be food to him.

Impiorum querela. —Augusties. —Varus. —Tiberius. —The complaint of Caligula was most wicked of the condition of his times, when he said they were not famous for any public calamity, as the reign of Augustus was, by the defeat of Varus and the legions; and that of Tiberius, by the falling of the theatre at Fidenae; whilst his oblivion was eminent through the prosperity of his affairs. As that other voice of his was worthier a headsman than a head when he wished the people of Rome had but one neck. But he found when he fell they had many hands. A tyrant, how great and mighty soever he may seem to cowards and sluggards, is but one creature, one animal.

Nobilium ingenia. —I have marked among the nobility some are so addicted to the service of the prince and commonwealth, as they look not for spoil; such are to be honoured and loved. There are others which no obligation will fasten on; and they are of two sorts. The first are such as love their own ease; or, out of vice, of nature, or self-direction, avoid business and care. Yet these the prince may use with safety. The other remove themselves upon craft and design, as the architects say, with a premeditated thought, to their own rather than their prince's profit. Such let the prince take heed of, and not doubt to reckon in the list of his open enemies.

Principum. varia. —Firmissima vero omnium basis jus haereditarium Principis. —There is a great variation between him that is raised to the sovereignty by the favour of his peers and him that comes to it by the suffrage of the people. The first holds with more difficulty, because he hath to do with many that think themselves his equals, and raised him for their own greatness and oppression of the rest. The latter hath no upbraiders, but was raised by them that sought to be defended from oppression: whose end is both easier and the honester to satisfy. Beside, while he hath the people to friend, who are a multitude, he hath the less fear of the nobility, who are but few. Nor let the common proverb (of he that builds on the people builds on the dirt) discredit my opinion: for that hath only place where an ambitious and private person, for some popular end, trusts in them against the public justice and magistrate. There they will leave him. But when a prince governs them, so as they have still need of his administrations (for that is his art), he shall ever make and hold them faithful.

Clementia. —Machiavell. —A prince should exercise his cruelty not by himself but by his ministers; so he may save himself and his dignity with his people by sacrificing those when he list, saith the great doctor of state, Machiavell. But I say he puts off man and goes into a beast, that is cruel. No virtue is a prince's own, or becomes him more, than this clemency: and no glory is greater than to be able to save with his power. Many punishments sometimes, and in some cases, as much discredit a prince, as many funerals a physician. The state of things is secured by clemency; severity represseth a few, but irritates more. {74a} The lopping of trees makes the boughs shoot out thicker; and the taking away of some kind of enemies increaseth the number. It is then most gracious in a prince to pardon when many about him would make him cruel; to think then how much he can save when others tell him how much he can destroy; not to consider what the impotence of others hath demolished, but what his own greatness can sustain. These are a prince's virtues: and they that give him other counsels are but the hangman's factors.

Clementia tutela optima. —He that is cruel to halves (saith the said St. Nicholas {74b}) loseth no less the opportunity of his cruelty than of his benefits: for then to use his cruelty is too late; and to use his favours will be interpreted fear and necessity, and so he loseth the thanks. Still the counsel is cruelty. But princes, by hearkening to cruel counsels, become in time obnoxious to the authors, their flatterers, and ministers; and are brought to that, that when they would, they dare not change them; they must go on and defend cruelty with cruelty; they cannot alter the habit. It is then grown necessary, they must be as ill as those have made them: and in the end they will grow more hateful to themselves than to their subjects. Whereas, on the contrary, the merciful prince is safe in love, not in fear. He needs no emissaries, spies, intelligencers to entrap true subjects. He fears no libels, no treasons. His people speak what they think, and talk openly what they do in secret. They have nothing in their breasts that they need a cypher for. He is guarded with his own benefits.

Religio. Palladium Homeri. —Euripides. —The strength of empire is in religion. What else is the Palladium (with Homer) that kept Troy so long from sacking? Nothing more commends the Sovereign to the subject than it. For he that is religious must be merciful and just necessarily: and they are two strong ties upon mankind. Justice the virtue that innocence rejoiceth in. Yet even that is not always so safe, but it may love to stand in the sight of mercy. For sometimes misfortune is made a crime, and then innocence is succoured no less than virtue. Nay, oftentimes virtue is made capital; and through the condition of the times it may happen that that may be punished with our praise. Let no man therefore murmur at the actions of the prince, who is placed so far above him. If he offend, he hath his discoverer. God hath a height beyond him. But where the prince is good, Euripides saith, "God is a guest in a human body. "

Tyranni. — Sejanus. — There is nothing with some princes sacred above their majesty, or profane, but what violates their sceptres. But a prince, with such a council, is like the god Terminus, of stone, his own landmark, or (as it is in the fable) a crowned lion. It is dangerous offending such a one, who, being angry, knows not how to forgive; that cares not to do anything for maintaining or enlarging of empire; kills not men or subjects, but destroyeth whole countries, armies, mankind, male and female, guilty or not guilty, holy or profane; yea, some that have not seen the light. All is under the law of their spoil and licence. But princes that neglect their proper office thus their fortune is oftentimes to draw a Sejanus to be near about them, who at last affect to get above them, and put them in a worthy fear of rooting both them out and their family. For no men hate an evil prince more than they that helped to make him such. And none more boastingly weep his ruin than they that procured and practised it. The same path leads to ruin which did to rule when men profess a licence in government. A good king is a public servant.

Illiteratus princeps. — A prince without letters is a pilot without eyes. All his government is groping. In sovereignty it is a most happy thing not to be compelled; but so it is the most miserable not to be counselled. And how can he be counselled that cannot see to read the best counsellors (which are books), for they neither flatter us nor hide from us? He may hear, you will say; but how shall he always be sure to hear truth, or be counselled the best things, not the sweetest? They say princes learn no art truly but the art of horsemanship. The reason is the brave beast is no flatterer. He will throw a prince as soon as his groom. Which is an argument that the good counsellors to princes are the best instruments of a good age. For though the prince himself be of a most prompt inclination to all virtue, yet the best pilots have needs of mariners besides sails, anchor, and other tackle.

Character principis. — Alexander magnus. — If men did know what shining fetters, gilded miseries, and painted happiness thrones and sceptres were there would not be so frequent strife about the getting or holding of them; there would be more principalities than princes; for a prince is the pastor of the people. He ought to shear, not to flay his sheep; to take their fleeces, not their the soul of the commonwealth, and ought to cherish it as his own body. Alexander the Great was wont to say, "He hated that gardener that plucked his herbs or flowers up by the roots. " A man may milk a beast till the blood come; churn milk and it yieldeth butter, but wring the nose and the blood followeth. He is an ill prince that so pulls his subjects' feathers as he would not have them grow again; that makes his exchequer a receipt for the spoils of those he governs. No, let him keep his own, not affect his subjects'; strive rather to be called just than powerful. Not, like the Roman tyrants, affect the surnames that grow by human slaughters; neither to seek war in peace, nor peace in war, but to observe faith given, though to an enemy. Study piety toward the subject; show care to defend him. Be slow to punish in divers cases, but be a sharp and severe revenger of open crimes. Break no decrees or dissolve no orders to slacken the strength of laws. Choose neither magistrates, civil or ecclesiastical, by favour or price; but with long disquisition and report of their worth by all suffrages. Sell no honours, nor give them hastily, but bestow them with counsel and for reward; if he do, acknowledge it (though late), and mend it. For princes are easy to be deceived; and what wisdom can escape where so many court-arts are studied? But, above all, the prince is to remember that when the great day of account comes, which neither magistrate nor prince can shun, there will be required of him a reckoning for those whom he hath trusted, as for himself, which he must provide. And if piety be wanting in the priests, equity in the judges, or the magistrates be found rated at a price, what justice or religion is to be expected? which are the only two attributes make kings akin to God, and is the Delphic sword, both to kill sacrifices and to chastise offenders.

De gratiosis. —When a virtuous man is raised, it brings gladness to his friends, grief to his enemies, and glory to his posterity. Nay, his honours are a great part of the honour of the times; when by this means he is grown to active men an example, to the slothful a spur, to the envious a punishment.

Divites. —Heredes ex asse. He which is sole heir to many rich men, having (besides his father's and uncle's) the estates of divers his kindred come to him by accession, must needs be richer than father or grandfather; so they which are left heirs ex asse of all their ancestors' vices, and by their good husbandry improve the old and daily purchase new, must needs be wealthier in vice, and have a greater revenue or stock of ill to spend on.

Fures publici. —The great thieves of a state are lightly the officers of the crown; they hang the less still, play the pikes in the pond, eat whom they list. The net was never spread for the hawk or buzzard that hurt us, but the harmless birds; they are good meat: -

"Dat veniam corvis, vexat censura columbas. " {81a}
"Non rete accipitri tenditur, neque milvio. " {81b}

Lewis XI. —But they are not always safe though, especially when they meet with wise masters. They can take down all the huff and swelling of their looks, and like dexterous auditors place the counter where he shall value nothing. Let them but remember Lewis XI., who to a Clerk of the Exchequer that came to be Lord Treasurer, and had (for his device) represented himself sitting on fortune's wheel, told him he might do well to fasten it with a good strong nail, lest, turning about, it might bring him where he was again. As indeed it did.

De bonis et malis. —De innocentia. —A good man will avoid the spot of any sin. The very aspersion is grievous, which makes him choose his way in his life as he would in his journey. The ill man rides through all confidently; he is coated and booted for it. The oftener he offends, the more openly, and the fouler, the fitter in fashion. His modesty, like a riding-coat, the more it is worn is the less cared for. It is good enough for the dirt still, and the ways he travels in. An innocent man needs no eloquence, his innocence is instead of it, else I had never come off so many times from these precipices, whither men's malice hath pursued me. It is true I have been accused to the lords, to the king, and by great ones, but it happened my accusers had not thought of the accusation with themselves, and so were driven, for want of crimes, to use invention, which was found slander, or too late (being entered so fair) to seek starting-holes for their rashness, which were not given them. And then they may think what accusation that was like to prove, when they that were the engineers feared to be the authors. Nor were they content to feign things against me, but to urge things, feigned by the ignorant, against my profession, which though, from their hired and mercenary impudence, I might have passed by as granted to a nation of barkers that let out their tongues to lick others' sores; yet I durst not leave myself undefended, having a pair of ears unskilful to hear lies, or have those things said of me which I could truly prove of them. They objected making of verses to me, when I could object to most of them, their not being able to read them, but as worthy of scorn. Nay, they would offer to urge mine own writings against me, but by pieces (which was an excellent way of malice), as if any man's context might not seem dangerous and offensive, if that which was knit to what went before were defrauded of his beginning; or that things by themselves uttered might not seem subject to calumny, which read entire would appear most free. At last they upbraided my poverty: I confess she is my domestic; sober of diet, simple of habit, frugal, painful, a good counseller to me, that keeps me from cruelty, pride, or other more delicate impertinences, which are the nurse-children of riches. But let them look over all the great and monstrous wickednesses, they shall never find those in poor families. They are the issue of the wealthy giants and the mighty hunters, whereas no great work, or worthy of praise or memory, but came out of poor cradles. It was the ancient poverty that founded commonweals, built cities, invented arts, made wholesome laws, armed men against vices, rewarded them with their own virtues, and preserved the honour and state of nations, till they betrayed themselves to riches.

Amor nummi. —Money never made any man rich, but his mind. He that can order himself to the law of Nature is not only without the sense but the fear of poverty. O! but to strike blind the people with our wealth and pomp is the thing! What a wretchedness is this, to thrust all our riches outward, and be beggars within; to contemplate nothing but the little, vile, and sordid things of the world; not the great, noble, and precious! We serve our avarice, and, not content with the good of the earth that is offered us, we search and dig for the evil that is hidden. God offered us those things, and placed them at hand, and near us, that He knew were profitable for us, but the hurtful He laid deep and hid. Yet do we seek only the things whereby we may perish, and bring them forth, when God and Nature hath buried them. We covet superfluous things, when it were more honour for us if we would contemn necessary. What need hath Nature of silver dishes, multitudes of waiters, delicate pages, perfumed napkins? She requires meat only, and hunger is not ambitious. Can we think no wealth enough but such a state for which a man may be brought into a premunire, begged, proscribed, or poisoned? O! if a man could restrain the fury of his gullet and groin, and think how many fires, how many kitchens, cooks, pastures, and ploughed lands; what orchards, stews, ponds and parks, coops and garners, he could spare; what velvets, tissues, embroideries, laces, he could lack; and then how short and uncertain his life is; he were in a better way to happiness than to live the emperor of these delights, and be the dictator of fashions; but we make ourselves slaves to our pleasures, and we serve fame and ambition, which is an equal slavery. Have not I seen the pomp of a whole kingdom, and what a foreign king could bring hither? Also to make himself gazed and wondered at—laid forth, as it were, to the show—and vanish all away in a day? And shall that which could not fill the expectation of few hours, entertain and take up our whole lives, when even it appeared as superfluous to the possessors as to me that was a spectator? The bravery was shown, it was not possessed; while it boasted itself it perished. It is vile, and a poor thing to place our happiness on these desires. Say we wanted them all. Famine ends famine.

De mollibus et effoeminatis. —There is nothing valiant or solid to be hoped for from such as are always kempt and perfumed, and every day smell of the tailor; the exceedingly curious that are wholly in mending such an imperfection in the face, in taking away the morphew in the neck, or bleaching their hands at midnight, gumming and bridling their beards, or making the waist small, binding it with hoops, while the mind runs at waste; too much pickedness is not manly. Not from those that will jest at their own outward imperfections, but hide their ulcers within, their pride, lust, envy, ill-nature, with all the art and authority they can. These persons are in danger, for whilst they think to justify their ignorance by impudence, and their persons by clothes and outward ornaments, they use but a commission to deceive themselves: where, if we will look with our understanding, and not our senses, we may behold virtue and beauty (though covered with rags) in their brightness; and vice and deformity so much the fouler, in having all the splendour of riches to gild them, or the false light of honour and power to help them. Yet this is that wherewith the world is taken, and runs mad to gaze on—clothes and titles, the birdlime of fools.

De stultitia. —What petty things they are we wonder at, like children that esteem every trifle, and prefer a fairing before their fathers! What difference is between us and them but that we are dearer fools, coxcombs at a higher rate? They are pleased with cockleshells, whistles, hobby-horses, and such like; we with statues, marble pillars, pictures, gilded roofs, where underneath is lath and lime, perhaps loam. Yet we take pleasure in the lie, and are glad we can cozen ourselves. Nor is it only in our walls and ceilings, but all that we call happiness is mere painting and gilt, and all for money. What a thin membrane of honour that is! and how hath all true reputation fallen, since money began to have any! Yet the great herd, the multitude, that in all other things are divided, in this alone conspire and agree—to love money. They wish for it, they embrace it, they adore it, while yet it is possessed with greater stir and torment than it is gotten.

De sibi molestis. —Some men what losses soever they have they make them greater, and if they have none, even all that is not gotten is a loss. Can there be creatures of more wretched condition than these, that continually labour under their own misery and others' envy? A man should study other things, not to covet, not to fear, not to repent him; to make his base such as no tempest shall shake him; to be secure of all opinion, and pleasing to himself, even for that wherein he displeaseth others; for the worst opinion gotten for doing well, should delight us. Wouldst not thou be just but for fame, thou oughtest to be it with infamy; he that would have his virtue published is not the servant of virtue, but glory.

Periculosa melancholia. —It is a dangerous thing when men's minds come to sojourn with their affections, and their diseases eat into their strength; that when too much desire and greediness of vice hath made the body unfit, or unprofitable, it is yet gladded with the sight and spectacle of it in others; and for want of ability to be an actor, is content to be a witness. It enjoys the pleasure of sinning in beholding others sin, as in dining, drinking, drabbing, &c. Nay, when it cannot do all these, it is offended with his own narrowness, that excludes it from the universal delights of mankind, and oftentimes dies of a melancholy, that it cannot be vicious enough.

Falsae species fugiendae. —I am glad when I see any man avoid the infamy of a vice; but to shun the vice itself were better. Till he do that he is but like the 'pientice, who, being loth to be spied by his master coming forth of Black Lucy's, went in again; to whom his master cried, "The more thou runnest that way to hide thyself, the more thou art in the place. " So are those that keep a tavern all day, that they may not be seen at night. I have known lawyers, divines—yea, great ones—of this heresy.

Decipimur specie. —There is a greater reverence had of things remote or strange to us than of much better if they be nearer and fall under our sense. Men, and almost all sorts of creatures, have their reputation by distance. Rivers, the farther they run, and more from their spring, the broader they are, and greater. And where our original is known, we are less the confident; among strangers we trust fortune. Yet a man may live as renowned at home, in his own country, or a private village, as in the whole world. For it is virtue that gives glory; that will endenizen a man everywhere. It is only that can naturalise him. A native, if he be vicious, deserves to be a stranger, and cast out of the commonwealth as an alien.

Dejectio Aulic. —A dejected countenance and mean clothes beget often a contempt, but it is with the shallowest creatures; courtiers commonly: look up even with them in a new suit, you get above them straight. Nothing is more short-lived than pride; it is but while their clothes last: stay but while these are worn out, you cannot wish the thing more wretched or dejected.

Poesis, et pictura. —Plutarch. Poetry and picture are arts of a like nature, and both are busy about imitation. It was excellently said of Plutarch, poetry was a speaking picture, and picture a mute poesy. For they both invent, feign and devise many things, and accommodate all they invent to the use and service of Nature. Yet of the two, the pen is more noble than the pencil; for that can speak to the understanding, the other but to the sense. They both behold pleasure and profit as their common object; but should abstain from all base pleasures, lest they should err from their end, and, while they seek to better men's minds, destroy their manners. They both are born artificers, not made. Nature is more powerful in them than study.

De pictura. —Whosoever loves not picture is injurious to truth and all the wisdom of poetry. Picture is the invention of heaven, the most ancient and most akin to Nature. It is itself a silent work, and always of one and the same habit; yet it doth so enter and penetrate the inmost affection (being done by an excellent artificer) as sometimes it overcomes the power of speech and oratory. There are divers graces in it, so are there in the artificers. One excels in care, another in reason, a third in easiness, a fourth in nature and grace. Some have diligence and comeliness, but they want majesty. They can express a human form in all the graces, sweetness, and elegancy, but, they miss the authority. They can hit nothing but smooth cheeks; they cannot express roughness or gravity. Others aspire to truth so much as they are rather lovers of likeness than beauty. Zeuxis and Parrhasius are said to be contemporaries; the first found out the reason of lights and shadows in picture, the other more subtlely examined the line.

De stylo. —Pliny. —In picture light is required no less than shadow; so in style, height as well as humbleness. But beware they be not too humble, as Pliny pronounced of Regulus's writings. You would think them written, not on a child, but by a child. Many, out of their own obscene apprehensions, refuse proper and fit words—as occupy, Nature, and the like; so the curious industry in some, of having all alike good, hath come nearer a vice than a virtue.

De progres. picturae. {93} Picture took her feigning from poetry; from geometry her rule, compass, lines, proportion, and the whole symmetry. Parrhasius was the first won reputation by adding symmetry to picture; he added subtlety to the countenance, elegancy to the hair, love-lines to the face, and by the public voice of all artificers, deserved honour in the outer lines. Eupompus gave it splendour by numbers and other elegancies. From the optics it drew reasons, by which it considered how things placed at distance and afar off should appear less; how above or beneath the head should deceive the eye, &c. So from thence it took shadows, recessor, light, and heightnings. From moral philosophy it took the soul, the expression of senses, perturbations, manners, when they would paint an angry person, a proud, an inconstant, an ambitious, a brave, a magnanimous, a just, a merciful, a compassionate, an humble, a dejected, a base, and the like; they made all heightnings bright, all shadows dark, all swellings from a plane, all solids from breaking. See where he complains of their painting Chimaeras {94} (by the vulgar unaptly called grotesque) saying that men who were born truly to study and emulate Nature did nothing but make monsters against Nature, which Horace so laughed at. {95} The art plastic was moulding in clay, or potter's earth anciently. This is the parent of statuary, sculpture, graving, and picture; cutting in brass and marble, all serve under her. Socrates taught Parrhasius and Clito (two noble statuaries) first to express manners by their looks in imagery. Polygnotus and Aglaophon were ancienter. After them Zeuxis, who was the lawgiver to all painters; after, Parrhasius. They were contemporaries, and lived both about Philip's time, the father of Alexander the Great. There lived in this latter age six famous painters in Italy, who were excellent and emulous of the ancients— Raphael de Urbino, Michael Angelo Buonarotti, Titian, Antony of Correggio, Sebastian of Venice, Julio Romano, and Andrea Sartorio.

Parasiti ad mensam. —These are flatterers for their bread, that praise all my oraculous lord does or says, be it true or false; invent tales that shall please; make baits for his lordship's ears; and if they be not received in what they offer at, they shift a point of the compass, and turn their tale, presently tack about, deny what they confessed, and confess what they denied; fit their discourse to the persons and occasions. What they snatch up and devour at one table, utter at another; and grow suspected of the master, hated of the servants, while they inquire, and reprehend, and compound, and dilate business of the house they have nothing to do with. They praise my lord's wine and the sauce he likes; observe the cook and bottle-man; while they stand in my lord's favour, speak for a pension for them, but pound them to dust upon my lord's least distaste, or change of his palate.

How much better is it to be silent, or at least to speak sparingly! for it is not enough to speak good, but timely things. If a man be asked a question, to answer; but to repeat the question before he answer is well, that he be sure to understand it, to avoid absurdity; for it is less dishonour to hear imperfectly than to speak imperfectly. The ears are excused, the understanding is not. And in things unknown to a man, not to give his opinion, lest by the affectation of knowing too much he lose the credit he hath, by speaking or knowing the wrong way what he utters. Nor seek to get his patron's favour by embarking himself in the factions of the family, to inquire after domestic simulties, their sports or affections. They are an odious and vile kind of creatures, that fly about the house all day, and picking up the filth of the house like pies or swallows, carry it to their nest (the lord's ears), and oftentimes report the lies they have feigned for what they have seen and heard,

Imo serviles. —These are called instruments of grace and power with great persons, but they are indeed the organs of their impotency, and marks of weakness. For sufficient lords are able to make these discoveries themselves. Neither will an honourable person inquire who eats and drinks together, what that man plays, whom this man loves, with whom such a one walks, what discourse they hold, who sleeps with whom. They are base and servile natures that busy themselves about these disquisitions. How often have I seen (and worthily) these censors of the family undertaken by some honest rustic and cudgelled thriftily! These are commonly the off-scouring and dregs of men that do these things, or calumniate others; yet I know not truly which is worse—he that maligns all, or that praises all. There is as a vice in praising, and as frequent, as in detracting.

It pleased your lordship of late to ask my opinion touching the education of your sons, and especially to the advancement of their studies. To which, though I returned somewhat for the present, which rather manifested a will in me than gave any just resolution to the thing propounded, I have upon better cogitation called those aids about me, both of mind and memory, which shall venture my thoughts clearer, if not fuller, to your lordship's demand. I confess, my lord, they will seem but petty and minute things I shall offer to you, being writ for children, and of them. But studies have their infancy as well as creatures. We see in men even the strongest compositions had their beginnings from milk and the cradle; and the wisest tarried sometimes about apting their mouths to letters and syllables. In their education, therefore, the care must be the greater had of their beginnings, to know, examine, and weigh their natures; which, though they be proner in some children to some disciplines, yet are they naturally prompt to taste all by degrees, and with change. For change is a kind of refreshing in studies, and infuseth knowledge by way of recreation. Thence the school itself is called a play or game, and all letters are so best taught to scholars. They should not be affrighted or deterred in their entry, but drawn on with exercise and emulation. A youth should not be made to hate study before he know the causes to love it, or taste the bitterness before the sweet; but called on and allured, entreated and praised — yea, when he deserves it not. For which cause I wish them sent to the best school, and a public, which I think the best. Your lordship, I fear, hardly hears of that, as willing to breed them in your eye and at home, and doubting their manners may be corrupted abroad. They are in more danger in your own family, among ill servants (allowing they be safe in their schoolmaster), than amongst a thousand boys, however immodest. Would we did not spoil our own children, and overthrow their manners ourselves by too much indulgence! To breed them at home is to breed them in a shade, whereas in a school they have the light and heat of the sun. They are used and accustomed to things and men. When they come forth into the common-wealth, they find nothing new, or to seek. They have made their friendships and aids, some to last their age. They hear what is commanded to others as well as themselves; much approved, much corrected; all which they bring to their own store and use, and learn as much as they hear. Eloquence would be but a poor thing if we should only converse with singulars, speak but man and man together. Therefore I like no private breeding. I would send them where their industry should be daily increased by praise, and that kindled by emulation. It is a good thing to inflame the mind; and though ambition itself be a vice, it is often the cause of great virtue. Give me that wit whom praise excites, glory puts on, or disgrace grieves; he is to be nourished with ambition, pricked forward with honour, checked with reprehension, and never to be suspected of sloth. Though he be given to play, it is a sign of spirit and liveliness, so there be a mean had of their sports and relaxations. And from the rod or ferule I would have them free, as from the menace of them; for it is both deformed and servile.

De stylo, et optimo scribendi genere. —For a man to write well, there are required three necessaries—to read the best authors, observe the best speakers, and much exercise of his own style; in style to consider what ought to be written, and after what manner. He must first think and excogitate his matter, then choose his words, and examine the weight of either. Then take care, in placing and ranking both matter and words, that the composition be comely; and to do this with diligence and often. No matter how slow the style be at first, so it be laboured and accurate; seek the best, and be not glad of the froward conceits, or first words, that offer themselves to us; but judge of what we invent, and order what we approve. Repeat often what we have formerly written; which beside that it helps the consequence, and makes the juncture better, it quickens the heat of imagination, that often cools in the time of setting down, and gives it new strength, as if it grew lustier by the going back; as we see in the contention of leaping, they jump farthest that fetch their race largest; or, as in throwing a dart or javelin, we force back our arms to make our loose the stronger. Yet, if we have a fair gale of wind, I forbid not the steering out of our sail, so the favour of the gale deceive us not. For all that we invent doth please us in conception of birth, else we would never set it down. But the safest is to return to our judgment, and handle over again those things the easiness of which might make them justly suspected. So did the best writers in their beginnings; they imposed upon themselves care and industry; they did nothing rashly: they obtained first to write well, and then custom made it easy and a habit. By little and little their matter showed itself to them more plentifully; their words answered, their composition followed; and all, as in a well-ordered family, presented itself in the place. So that the sum of all is, ready writing makes not good writing, but good writing brings on ready writing yet, when we think we have got the faculty, it is even then good to resist it, as to give a horse a check sometimes with a bit, which doth not so much stop his course as stir his mettle. Again, whether a man's genius is best able to reach thither, it should more and more contend, lift and dilate itself, as men of low stature raise themselves on their toes, and so ofttimes get even, if not eminent. Besides, as it is fit for grown and able writers to stand of themselves, and work with their own strength, to trust and endeavour by their own faculties, so it is fit for the beginner and learner to study others and the best. For the mind and memory are more sharply exercised in comprehending another man's things than our own; and such as accustom themselves and are familiar with the best authors shall ever and anon find somewhat of them in themselves, and in the expression of their minds, even when they feel it not, be able to utter something like theirs, which hath an authority above their own. Nay, sometimes it is the reward of a man's study, the praise of quoting another man fitly; and though a man be more prone and able for one kind of writing than another, yet he must exercise all. For as in an instrument, so in style, there must be a harmony and consent of parts.

Praecipiendi modi. —I take this labour in teaching others, that they should not be always to be taught, and I would bring my precepts into practice, for rules are ever of less force and value than experiments; yet with this purpose, rather to show the right way to those that come after, than to detect any that have slipped before by error, and I hope it will be more profitable. For men do more willingly listen, and with more favour, to precept, than reprehension. Among divers opinions of an art, and most of them contrary in themselves, it is hard to make election; and, therefore, though a man cannot invent new things after so many, he may do a welcome work yet to help posterity to judge rightly of the old. But arts and precepts avail nothing, except Nature be beneficial and aiding. And therefore these things are no more written to a dull disposition, than rules of husbandry to a soil. No precepts will profit a fool, no more than beauty will the blind, or music the deaf. As we should take care that our style in writing be neither dry nor empty, we should look again it be not winding, or wanton with far-fetched descriptions; either is a vice. But that is worse which proceeds out of want, than that which riots out of plenty. The remedy of fruitfulness is easy, but no labour will help the contrary; I will like and praise some things in a young writer which yet, if he continue in, I cannot but justly hate him for the same. There is a time to be given all things for maturity, and that even your country husband-man can teach, who to a young plant will not put the pruning-knife, because it seems to fear the iron, as not able to admit the scar. No more would I tell a green writer all his faults, lest I should make him grieve and faint, and at last despair; for nothing doth more hurt than to make him so afraid of all things as he can endeavour nothing. Therefore youth ought to be instructed betimes, and in the best things; for we hold those longest we take soonest, as the first scent of a vessel lasts, and the tint the wool first receives; therefore a master should temper his own powers, and descend to the other's infirmity. If you pour a glut of water upon a bottle, it receives little of it; but with a funnel, and by degrees, you shall fill many of them, and spill little of your own; to their capacity they will all receive and be full. And as it is fit to read the best authors to youth first, so let them be of the openest and clearest. {106a} As Livy before Sallust, Sidney before Donne; and beware of letting them taste Gower or Chaucer at first, lest, falling too much in love with antiquity, and not apprehending the weight, they grow rough and barren in language only. When their judgments are firm, and out of danger, let them read both the old and the new; but no less take heed that their new flowers and sweetness do not as much corrupt as the others' dryness and squalor, if they choose not carefully. Spenser, in affecting the ancients, writ no language; yet I would have him read for his matter, but as Virgil read Ennius. The reading of Homer and Virgil is counselled by Quintilian as the best way of informing youth and confirming man. For, besides that the mind is raised with the height and sublimity of such a verse, it takes spirit from the greatness of the matter, and is tinctured with the best things. Tragic and lyric poetry is good, too, and comic with the best, if the manners of the reader be once in safety. In the Greek poets, as also in Plautus, we shall see the economy and disposition of poems better observed than in Terence; and the latter, who thought the sole grace and virtue of their fable the sticking in of sentences, as ours do the forcing in of jests.

Fals. querel. fugiend. Platonis peregrinatio in Italiam. —We should not protect our sloth with the patronage of difficulty. It is a false quarrel against Nature, that she helps understanding but in a few, when the most part of mankind are inclined by her thither, if they would take the pains; no less than birds to fly, horses to run, &c., which if they lose, it is through their own sluggishness, and by that means become her prodigies, not her children. I confess, Nature in children is more patient of labour in study than in age; for the sense of the pain, the judgment of the labour is absent; they do not measure what they have done. And it is the thought and consideration that affects us more than the weariness itself. Plato was not content with the learning that Athens could give him, but sailed into Italy, for Pythagoras' knowledge: and yet not thinking himself sufficiently informed, went into Egypt, to the priests, and learned their mysteries. He laboured, so must we. Many things may be learned together, and performed in one point of time; as musicians exercise their memory, their voice, their fingers, and sometimes their head and feet at once. And so a preacher, in the invention of matter, election of words, composition of gesture, look, pronunciation, motion, useth all these faculties at once: and if we can express this variety together, why should not divers studies, at divers hours, delight, when the variety is able alone to refresh and repair us? As, when a man is weary of writing, to read; and then again of reading, to write. Wherein, howsoever we do many things, yet are we (in a sort) still fresh to what we begin; we are recreated with change, as the stomach is with meats. But some will say this variety breeds confusion, and makes, that either we lose all, or hold no more than the last. Why do we not then persuade husbandmen that they should not till land, help it with marl, lime, and compost? plant hop-gardens, prune trees, look to bee-hives, rear sheep, and all other cattle at once? It is easier to do many things and continue, than to do one thing long.

Praecept. element. —It is not the passing through these learnings that hurts us, but the dwelling and sticking about them. To descend to those extreme anxieties and foolish cavils of grammarians, is able to break a wit in pieces, being a work of manifold misery and vainness, to be elementarii senes. Yet even letters are, as it were, the bank of words, and restore themselves to an author as the pawns of language: but talking and eloquence are not the same: to speak, and to speak well, are two things. A fool may talk, but a wise man speaks; and out of the observation, knowledge, and the use of things, many writers perplex their readers and hearers with mere nonsense. Their writings need sunshine. Pure and neat language I love, yet plain and customary. A barbarous phrase has often made me out of love with a good sense, and doubtful writing hath wracked me beyond my patience. The reason why a poet is said that he ought to have all knowledges is, that he should not be ignorant of the most, especially of those he will handle. And indeed, when the attaining of them is possible, it were a sluggish and base thing to despair; for frequent imitation of anything becomes a habit quickly. If a man should prosecute as much as could be said of everything, his work would find no end.

De orationis dignitate. [Greek text]. —Metaphora. Speech is the only benefit man hath to express his excellency of mind above other creatures. It is the instrument of society; therefore Mercury, who is the president of language, is called deorum hominumque interpres. {110a} In all speech, words and sense are as the body and the soul. The sense is as the life and soul of language, without which all words are dead. Sense is wrought out of experience, the knowledge of human life and actions, or of the liberal arts, which the Greeks called [Greek text]. Words are the people's, yet there is a choice of them to be made; for verborum delectus origo est eloquentiae. {111a} They are to be chosen according to the persons we make speak, or the things we speak of. Some are of the camp, some of the council-board, some of the shop, some of the sheepcote, some of the pulpit, some of the Bar, &c. And herein is seen their elegance and propriety, when we use them fitly and draw them forth to their just strength and nature by way of translation or metaphor. But in this translation we must only serve necessity (nam temere nihil transfertur a prudenti) {111b} or commodity, which is a kind of necessity: that is, when we either absolutely want a word to express by, and that is necessity; or when we have not so fit a word, and that is commodity; as when we avoid loss by it, and escape obsceneness, and gain in the grace and property which helps significance. Metaphors far-fetched hinder to be understood; and affected, lose their grace. Or when the person fetcheth his translations from a wrong place as if a privy councillor should at the table take his metaphor from a dicing-house, or ordinary, or a vintner's vault; or a justice of peace draw his similitudes from the mathematics, or a divine from a bawdy house, or taverns; or a gentleman of Northamptonshire, Warwickshire, or the Midland, should fetch all the illustrations to his country neighbours from shipping, and tell them of the main-sheet and the bowline. Metaphors are thus many times deformed, as in him that said, Castratam morte Africani rempublicam; and another, Stercus curiae Glauciam, and Cana nive conspuit Alpes. All attempts that are new in this kind, are dangerous, and somewhat hard, before they be softened with use. A man coins not a new word without some peril and less fruit; for if it happen to be received, the praise is but moderate; if refused, the scorn is assured. Yet we must adventure; for things at first hard and rough are by use made tender and gentle. It is an honest error that is committed, following great chiefs.

Consuetudo. —Perspicuitas, Venustas. —Authoritas. —Virgil. — Lucretius. —Chaucerism. —Paronomasia. —Custom is the most certain mistress of language, as the public stamp makes the current money. But we must not be too frequent with the mint, every day coining, nor fetch words from the extreme and utmost ages; since the chief virtue of a style is perspicuity, and nothing so vicious in it as to need an interpreter. Words borrowed of antiquity do lend a kind of majesty to style, and are not without their delight sometimes; for they have the authority of years, and out of their intermission do win themselves a kind of grace like newness. But the eldest of the present, and newness of the past language, is the best. For what was the ancient language, which some men so dote upon, but the ancient custom? Yet when I name custom, I understand not the vulgar custom; for that were a precept no less dangerous to language than life, if we should speak or live after the manners of the vulgar: but that I call custom of speech, which is the consent of the learned; as custom of life, which is the consent of the good. Virgil was most loving of antiquity; yet how rarely doth he insert aquai and pictai! Lucretius is scabrous and rough in these; he seeks them: as some do Chaucerisms with us, which were better expunged and banished. Some words are to be culled out for ornament and colour, as we gather flowers to strew houses or make garlands; but they are better when they grow to our style; as in a meadow, where, though the mere grass and greenness delight, yet the variety of flowers doth heighten and beautify. Marry, we must not play or riot too much with them, as in Paronomasies; nor use too swelling or ill-sounding words! Quae per salebras, altaque saxa cadunt. {114a} It is true, there is no sound but shall find some lovers, as the bitterest confections are grateful to some palates. Our composition must be more accurate in the beginning and end than in the midst, and in the end more than in the beginning; for through the midst the stream bears us. And this is attained by custom, more than care of diligence. We must express readily and fully, not profusely. There is difference between a liberal and prodigal hand. As it is a great point of art, when our matter requires it, to enlarge and veer out all sail, so to take it in and contract it, is of no less praise, when the argument doth ask it. Either of them hath their fitness in the place. A good man always profits by his endeavour, by his help, yea, when he is absent; nay, when he is dead, by his example and memory. So good authors in their style: a strict and succinct style is that where you can take away nothing without loss, and that loss to be manifest.

De Stylo. —Tracitus. —The Laconic. —Suetonius. —Seneca and Fabianus. —The brief style is that which expresseth much in little; the concise style, which expresseth not enough, but leaves somewhat to be understood; the abrupt style, which hath many breaches, and doth not seem to end, but fall. The congruent and harmonious fitting of parts in a sentence hath almost the fastening and force of knitting and connection; as in stones well squared, which will rise strong a great way without mortar.

Periodi. —Obscuritas offundit tenebras. —Superlatio. —Periods are beautiful when they are not too long; for so they have their strength too, as in a pike or javelin. As we must take the care that our words and sense be clear, so if the obscurity happen through the hearer's or reader's want of understanding, I am not to answer for them, no more than for their not listening or marking; I must neither find them ears nor mind. But a man cannot put a word so in sense but something about it will illustrate it, if the writer understand himself; for order helps much to perspicuity, as confusion hurts. (Rectitudo lucem adfert; obliquitas et circumductio offuscat. {116a}) We should therefore speak what we can the nearest way, so as we keep our gait, not leap; for too short may as well be not let into the memory, as too long not kept in. Whatsoever loseth the grace and clearness, converts into a riddle; the obscurity is marked, but not the value. That perisheth, and is passed by, like the pearl in the fable. Our style should be like a skein of silk, to be carried and found by the right thread, not ravelled and perplexed; then all is a knot, a heap. There are words that do as much raise a style as others can depress it. Superlation and over-muchness amplifies; it may be above faith, but never above a mean. It was ridiculous in Cestius, when he said of Alexander:

"Fremit oceanus, quasi indignetur, quod terras relinquas. " {117a}

But propitiously from Virgil:

> "Credas innare revulsas
> Cycladas. " {117b}

He doth not say it was so, but seemed to be so. Although it be somewhat incredible, that is excused before it be spoken. But there are hyperboles which will become one language, that will by no means admit another. As Eos esse P. R. exercitus, qui caelum possint perrumpere, {118a} who would say with us, but a madman? Therefore we must consider in every tongue what is used, what received. Quintilian warns us, that in no kind of translation, or metaphor, or allegory, we make a turn from what we began; as if we fetch the original of our metaphor from sea and billows, we end not in flames and ashes: it is a most foul inconsequence. Neither must we draw out our allegory too long, lest either we make ourselves obscure, or fall into affectation, which is childish. But why do men depart at all from the right and natural ways of speaking? sometimes for necessity, when we are driven, or think it fitter, to speak that in obscure words, or by circumstance, which uttered plainly would offend the hearers. Or to avoid obsceneness, or sometimes for pleasure, and variety, as travellers turn out of the highway, drawn either by the commodity of a footpath, or the delicacy or freshness of the fields. And all this is called [Greek text] or figured language.

Oratio imago animi. —Language most shows a man: Speak, that I may see thee. It springs out of the most retired and inmost parts of us, and is the image of the parent of it, the mind. No glass renders a man's form or likeness so true as his speech. Nay, it is likened to a man; and as we consider feature and composition in a man, so words in language; in the greatness, aptness, sound structure, and harmony of it.

Structura et statura, sublimis, humilis, pumila. —Some men are tall and big, so some language is high and great. Then the words are chosen, their sound ample, the composition full, the absolution plenteous, and poured out, all grave, sinewy, and strong. Some are little and dwarfs; so of speech, it is humble and low, the words poor and flat, the members and periods thin and weak, without knitting or number.

Mediocris plana et placida. —The middle are of a just stature. There the language is plain and pleasing; even without stopping, round without swelling: all well-turned, composed, elegant, and accurate.

Vitiosa oratio, vasta—tumens—enormis—affectata—abjecta. —The vicious language is vast and gaping, swelling and irregular: when it contends to be high, full of rock, mountain, and pointedness; as it affects to be low, it is abject, and creeps, full of bogs and holes. And according to their subject these styles vary, and lose their names: for that which is high and lofty, declaring excellent matter, becomes vast and tumorous, speaking of petty and inferior things; so that which was even and apt in a mean and plain subject, will appear most poor and humble in a high argument. Would you not laugh to meet a great councillor of State in a flat cap, with his trunk hose, and a hobbyhorse cloak, his gloves under his girdle, and yond haberdasher in a velvet gown, furred with sables? There is a certain latitude in these things, by which we find the degrees.

Figura. —The next thing to the stature, is the figure and feature in language—that is, whether it be round and straight, which consists of short and succinct periods, numerous and polished; or square and firm, which is to have equal and strong parts everywhere answerable, and weighed.

Cutis sive cortex. Compositio. —The third is the skin and coat, which rests in the well-joining, cementing, and coagmentation of words; whenas it is smooth, gentle, and sweet, like a table upon which you may run your finger without rubs, and your nail cannot find a joint; not horrid, rough, wrinkled, gaping, or chapped: after these, the flesh, blood, and bones come in question.

Carnosa—adipata—redundans. —We say it is a fleshy style, when there is much periphrasis, and circuit of words; and when with more than enough, it grows fat and corpulent: arvina orationis, full of suet and tallow. It hath blood and juice when the words are proper and apt, their sound sweet, and the phrase neat and picked—oratio uncta, et bene pasta. But where there is redundancy, both the blood and juice are faulty and vicious: - Redundat sanguine, quia multo plus dicit, quam necesse est. Juice in language is somewhat less than blood; for if the words be but becoming and signifying, and the sense gentle, there is juice; but where that wanteth, the language is thin, flagging, poor, starved, scarce covering the bone, and shows like stones in a sack.

Jejuna, macilenta, strigosa. —Ossea, et nervosa. —Some men, to avoid redundancy, run into that; and while they strive to have no ill blood or juice, they lose their good. There be some styles, again, that have not less blood, but less flesh and corpulence. These are bony and sinewy; Ossa habent, et nervos.

Notae domini Sti. Albani de doctrin. intemper. —Dictator. —Aristoteles. —It was well noted by the late Lord St. Albans, that the study of words is the first distemper of learning; vain matter the second; and a third distemper is deceit, or the likeness of truth: imposture held up by credulity. All these are the cobwebs of learning, and to let them grow in us is either sluttish or foolish. Nothing is more ridiculous than to make an author a dictator, as the schools have done Aristotle. The damage is infinite knowledge receives by it; for to many things a man should owe but a temporary belief, and suspension of his own judgment, not an absolute resignation of himself, or a perpetual captivity. Let Aristotle and others have their dues; but if we can make farther discoveries of truth and fitness than they, why are we envied? Let us beware, while we strive to add, we do not diminish or deface; we may improve, but not augment. By discrediting falsehood, truth grows in request. We must not go about, like men anguished and perplexed, for vicious affectation of praise, but calmly study the separation of opinions, find the errors have intervened, awake antiquity, call former times into question; but make no parties with the present, nor follow any fierce undertakers, mingle no matter of doubtful credit with the simplicity of truth, but gently stir the mould about the root of the question, and avoid all digladiations, facility of credit, or superstitious simplicity, seek the consonancy and concatenation of truth; stoop only to point of necessity, and what leads to convenience. Then make exact animadversion where style hath degenerated, where flourished and thrived in choiceness of phrase, round and clean composition of sentence, sweet falling of the clause, varying an illustration by tropes and figures, weight of matter, worth of subject, soundness of argument, life of invention, and depth of judgment. This is monte potiri, to get the hill; for no perfect discovery can be made upon a flat or a level.

De optimo scriptore. —Cicero. —Now that I have informed you in the knowing of these things, let me lead you by the hand a little farther, in the direction of the use, and make you an able writer by practice. The conceits of the mind are pictures of things, and the tongue is the interpreter of those pictures. The order of God's creatures in themselves is not only admirable and glorious, but eloquent: then he who could apprehend the consequence of things in their truth, and utter his apprehensions as truly, were the best writer or speaker. Therefore Cicero said much, when he said, Dicere recte nemo potest, nisi qui prudenter intelligit. {124a} The shame of speaking unskilfully were small if the tongue only thereby were disgraced; but as the image of a king in his seal ill-represented is not so much a blemish to the wax, or the signet that sealed it, as to the prince it representeth, so disordered speech is not so much injury to the lips that give it forth, as to the disproportion and incoherence of things in themselves, so negligently expressed. Neither can his mind be thought to be in tune, whose words do jar; nor his reason in frame, whose sentence is preposterous; nor his elocution clear and perfect, whose utterance breaks itself into fragments and uncertainties. Were it not a dishonour to a mighty prince, to have the majesty of his embassage spoiled by a careless ambassador? and is it not as great an indignity, that an excellent conceit and capacity, by the indiligence of an idle tongue, should be disgraced? Negligent speech doth not only discredit the person of the speaker, but it discrediteth the opinion of his reason and judgment; it discrediteth the force and uniformity of the matter and substance. If it be so then in words, which fly and escape censure, and where one good phrase begs pardon for many incongruities and faults, how shall he then be thought wise whose penning is thin and shallow? how shall you look for wit from him whose leisure and head, assisted with the examination of his eyes, yield you no life or sharpness in his writing?

De stylo epistolari. —Inventio. —In writing there is to be regarded the invention and the fashion. For the invention, that ariseth upon your business, whereof there can be no rules of more certainty, or precepts of better direction given, than conjecture can lay down from the several occasions of men's particular lives and vocations: but sometimes men make baseness of kindness: As "I could not satisfy myself till I had discharged my remembrance, and charged my letters with commendation to you; " or, "My business is no other than to testify my love to you, and to put you in mind of my willingness to do you all kind offices; " or, "Sir, have you leisure to descend to the remembering of that assurance you have long possessed in your servant, and upon your next opportunity make him happy with some commands from you? " or the like; that go a-begging for some meaning, and labour to be delivered of the great burden of nothing. When you have invented, and that your business be matter, and not bare form, or mere ceremony, but some earnest, then are you to proceed to the ordering of it, and digesting the parts, which is had out of two circumstances. One is the understanding of the persons to whom you are to write; the other is the coherence of your sentence; for men's capacity to weigh what will be apprehended with greatest attention or leisure; what next regarded and longed for especially, and what last will leave satisfaction, and (as it were) the sweetest memorial and belief of all that is passed in his understanding whom you write to. For the consequence of sentences, you must be sure that every clause do give the cue one to the other, and be bespoken ere it come. So much for invention and order.

Modus. —1. Brevitas. —Now for fashion: it consists in four things, which are qualities of your style. The first is brevity; for they must not be treatises or discourses (your letters) except it be to learned men. And even among them there is a kind of thrift and saving of words. Therefore you are to examine the clearest passages of your understanding, and through them to convey the sweetest and most significant words you can devise, that you may the easier teach them the readiest way to another man's apprehension, and open their meaning fully, roundly, and distinctly, so as the reader may not think a second view cast away upon your letter. And though respect be a part following this, yet now here, and still I must remember it, if you write to a man, whose estate and sense, as senses, you are familiar with, you may the bolder (to set a task to his brain) venture on a knot. But if to your superior, you are bound to measure him in three farther points: first, with interest in him; secondly, his capacity in your letters; thirdly, his leisure to peruse them. For your interest or favour with him, you are to be the shorter or longer, more familiar or submiss, as he will afford you time. For his capacity, you are to be quicker and fuller of those reaches and glances of wit or learning, as he is able to entertain them. For his leisure, you are commanded to the greater briefness, as his place is of greater discharges and cares. But with your betters, you are not to put riddles of wit, by being too scarce of words; not to cause the trouble of making breviates by writing too riotous and wastingly. Brevity is attained in matter by avoiding idle compliments, prefaces, protestations, parentheses, superfluous circuit of figures and digressions: in the composition, by omitting conjunctions [not only, but also; both the one and the other, whereby it cometh to pass] and such like idle particles, that have no great business in a serious letter but breaking of sentences, as oftentimes a short journey is made long by unnessary baits.

Quintilian. —But, as Quintilian saith, there is a briefness of the parts sometimes that makes the whole long: "As I came to the stairs, I took a pair of oars, they launched out, rowed apace, I landed at the court gate, I paid my fare, went up to the presence, asked for my lord, I was admitted. " All this is but, "I went to the court and spake with my lord. " This is the fault of some Latin writers within these last hundred years of my reading, and perhaps Seneca may be appeached of it; I accuse him not.

2. Perspicuitas. —The next property of epistolary style is perspicuity, and is oftentimes by affectation of some wit ill angled for, or ostentation of some hidden terms of art. Few words they darken speech, and so do too many; as well too much light hurteth the eyes, as too little; and a long bill of chancery confounds the understanding as much as the shortest note; therefore, let not your letters be penned like English statutes, and this is obtained. These vices are eschewed by pondering your business well and distinctly concerning yourself,

which is much furthered by uttering your thoughts, and letting them as well come forth to the light and judgment of your own outward senses as to the censure of other men's ears; for that is the reason why many good scholars speak but fumblingly; like a rich man, that for want of particular note and difference can bring you no certain ware readily out of his shop. Hence it is that talkative shallow men do often content the hearers more than the wise. But this may find a speedier redress in writing, where all comes under the last examination of the eyes. First, mind it well, then pen it, then examine it, then amend it, and you may be in the better hope of doing reasonably well. Under this virtue may come plainness, which is not to be curious in the order as to answer a letter, as if you were to answer to interrogatories. As to the first, first; and to the second, secondly, &c. but both in method to use (as ladies do in their attire) a diligent kind of negligence, and their sportive freedom; though with some men you are not to jest, or practise tricks; yet the delivery of the most important things may be carried with such a grace, as that it may yield a pleasure to the conceit of the reader. There must be store, though no excess of terms; as if you are to name store, sometimes you may call it choice, sometimes plenty, sometimes copiousness, or variety; but ever so, that the word which comes in lieu have not such difference of meaning as that it may put the sense of the first in hazard to be mistaken. You are not to cast a ring for the perfumed terms of the time, as accommodation, complement, spirit &c., but use them properly in their place, as others.

3. Vigor—There followeth life and quickness, which is the strength and sinews, as it were, of your penning by pretty sayings, similitudes, and conceits; allusions from known history, or other common-place, such as are in the Courtier, and the second book of Cicero De Oratore.

4. Discretio. —The last is, respect to discern what fits yourself, him to whom you write, and that which you handle, which is a quality fit to conclude the rest, because it doth include all. And that must proceed from ripeness of judgment, which, as one truly saith, is gotten by four means, God, nature, diligence, and conversation. Serve the first well, and the rest will serve you.

De Poetica. —We have spoken sufficiently of oratory, let us now make a diversion to poetry. Poetry, in the primogeniture, had many peccant humours, and is made to have more now, through the levity and inconstancy of men's judgments. Whereas, indeed, it is the most prevailing eloquence, and of the most exalted caract. Now the discredits and disgraces are many it hath received through men's study of depravation or calumny; their practice being to give it diminution of credit, by lessening the professor's estimation, and making the age afraid of their liberty; and the age is grown so tender of her fame, as she calls all writings aspersions.

That is the state word, the phrase of court (placentia college), which some call Parasites place, the Inn of Ignorance.

D. Hieronymus. —Whilst I name no persons, but deride follies, why should any man confess or betray himself why doth not that of S. Hierome come into their mind, Ubi generalis est de vitiis disputatio, ibi nullius esse personae injuriam? {133a} Is it such an inexpiable crime in poets to tax vices generally, and no offence in them, who, by their exception confess they have committed them particularly? Are we fallen into those times that we must not -

"Auriculas teneras mordaci rodere vero. " {133b}

Remedii votum semper verius erat, quam spes. {133c}—Sexus faemin. — If men may by no means write freely, or speak truth, but when it offends not, why do physicians cure with sharp medicines, or corrosives? is not the same equally lawful in the cure of the mind that is in the cure of the body? Some vices, you will say, are so foul that it is better they should be done than spoken. But they that take offence where no name, character, or signature doth blazon them seem to me like affected as women, who if they hear anything ill spoken of the ill of their sex, are presently moved, as if the contumely respected their particular; and on the contrary, when they hear good of good women, conclude that it belongs to them all. If I see anything that toucheth me, shall I come forth a betrayer of myself presently? No, if I be wise, I'll dissemble it; if honest, I'll avoid it, lest I publish that on my own forehead which I saw there noted without a title. A man that is on the mending hand will either ingenuously confess or wisely dissemble his disease. And the wise and virtuous will never think anything belongs to themselves that is written, but rejoice that the good are warned not to be such; and the ill to leave to be such. The person offended hath no reason to be offended with the writer, but with himself; and so to declare that properly to belong to him which was so spoken of all men, as it could be no man's several, but his that would wilfully and desperately claim it. It sufficeth I know what kind of persons I displease, men bred in the declining

53

and decay of virtue, betrothed to their own vices; that have abandoned or prostituted their good names; hungry and ambitious of infamy, invested in all deformity, enthralled to ignorance and malice, of a hidden and concealed malignity, and that hold a concomitancy with all evil.

What is a Poet?

Poeta. —A poet is that which by the Greeks is called [Greek text], a maker, or a feigner: his art, an art of imitation or feigning; expressing the life of man in fit measure, numbers, and harmony, according to Aristotle; from the word [Greek text], which signifies to make or feign. Hence he is called a poet, not he which writeth in measure only, but that feigneth and formeth a fable, and writes things like the truth. For the fable and fiction is, as it were, the form and soul of any poetical work or poem.

What mean, you by a Poem?

Poema. —A poem is not alone any work or composition of the poet's in many or few verses; but even one verse alone sometimes makes a perfect poem. As when AEneas hangs up and consecrates the arms of Abas with this inscription: -

"AEneas haec de Danais victoribus arma. " {136a}

And calls it a poem or carmen. Such are those in Martial: -

"Omnia, Castor, emis: sic fiet, ut omnia vendas. " {136b}

And -

"Pauper videri Cinna vult, et est pauper. " {136c}

Horatius. —Lucretius. —So were Horace's odes called Carmina, his lyric songs. And Lucretius designs a whole book in his sixth: -

"Quod in primo quoque carmine claret. " {136d}

Epicum. —Dramaticum. —Lyricum. —Elegiacum. —Epigrammat. — And anciently all the oracles were called Carmina; or whatever sentence was expressed, were it much or little, it was called an Epic, Dramatic, Lyric, Elegiac, or Epigrammatic poem.

Discoveries Made Upon Men and Matter and Some Poems

But how differs a Poem from what we call Poesy?

Poesis. —Artium regina. —Poet. differentiae. —Grammatic. —Logic. — Rhetoric. —Ethica. —A poem, as I have told you, is the work of the poet; the end and fruit of his labour and study. Poesy is his skill or craft of making; the very fiction itself, the reason or form of the work. And these three voices differ, as the thing done, the doing, and the doer; the thing feigned, the feigning, and the feigner; so the poem, the poesy, and the poet. Now the poesy is the habit or the art; nay, rather the queen of arts, which had her original from heaven, received thence from the Hebrews, and had in prime estimation with the Greeks transmitted to the Latins and all nations that professed civility. The study of it (if we will trust Aristotle) offers to mankind a certain rule and pattern of living well and happily, disposing us to all civil offices of society. If we will believe Tully, it nourisheth and instructeth our youth, delights our age, adorns our prosperity, comforts our adversity, entertains us at home, keeps us company abroad, travels with us, watches, divides the times of our earnest and sports, shares in our country recesses and recreations; insomuch as the wisest and best learned have thought her the absolute mistress of manners and nearest of kin to virtue. And whereas they entitle philosophy to be a rigid and austere poesy, they have, on the contrary, styled poesy a dulcet and gentle philosophy, which leads on and guides us by the hand to action with a ravishing delight and incredible sweetness. But before we handle the kinds of poems, with their special differences, or make court to the art itself, as a mistress, I would lead you to the knowledge of our poet by a perfect information what he is or should be by nature, by exercise, by imitation, by study, and so bring him down through the disciplines of grammar, logic, rhetoric, and the ethics, adding somewhat out of all, peculiar to himself, and worthy of your admittance or reception.

1. Ingenium. —Seneca. —Plato. —Aristotle. —Helicon. —Pegasus. — Parnassus. —Ovid. —First, we require in our poet or maker (for that title our language affords him elegantly with the Greek) a goodness of natural wit. For whereas all other arts consist of doctrine and precepts, the poet must be able by nature and instinct to pour out the treasure of his mind, and as Seneca saith, Aliquando secundum Anacreontem insanire jucundum esse; by which he understands the poetical rapture. And according to that of Plato, Frustra poeticas fores sui compos pulsavit. And of Aristotle, Nullum magnum ingenium sine mixtura dementiae fuit. Nec potest grande aliquid, et supra caeteros loqui, nisi mota mens. Then it riseth higher, as by a

divine instinct, when it contemns common and known conceptions. It utters somewhat above a mortal mouth. Then it gets aloft and flies away with his rider, whither before it was doubtful to ascend. This the poets understood by their Helicon, Pegasus, or Parnassus; and this made Ovid to boast,

> "Est deus in nobis, agitante calescimus illo
> Sedibus aethereis spiritus ille venit. " {139a}

Lipsius. —Petron. in. Fragm. —And Lipsius to affirm, Scio, poetam neminem praestantem fuisse, sine parte quadam uberiore divinae aurae. And hence it is that the coming up of good poets (for I mind not mediocres or imos) is so thin and rare among us. Every beggarly corporation affords the State a mayor or two bailiffs yearly; but Solus rex, aut poeta, non quotannis nascitur. To this perfection of nature in our poet we require exercise of those parts, and frequent.

2. Exercitatio. —Virgil. —Scaliger. —Valer. Maximus. —Euripides. — Alcestis. —If his wit will not arrive suddenly at the dignity of the ancients, let him not yet fall out with it, quarrel, or be over hastily angry; offer to turn it away from study in a humour, but come to it again upon better cogitation; try another time with labour. If then it succeed not, cast not away the quills yet, nor scratch the wainscot, beat not the poor desk, but bring all to the forge and file again; torn it anew. There is no statute law of the kingdom bids you be a poet against your will or the first quarter; if it comes in a year or two, it is well. The common rhymers pour forth verses, such as they are, ex tempore; but there never comes from them one sense worth the life of a day. A rhymer and a poet are two things. It is said of the incomparable Virgil that he brought forth his verses like a bear, and after formed them with licking. Scaliger the father writes it of him, that he made a quantity of verses in the morning, which afore night he reduced to a less number. But that which Valerius Maximus hath left recorded of Euripides, the tragic poet, his answer to Alcestis, another poet, is as memorable as modest; who, when it was told to Alcestis that Euripides had in three days brought forth but three verses, and those with some difficulty and throes, Alcestis, glorying he could with ease have sent forth a hundred in the space, Euripides roundly replied, "Like enough; but here is the difference: thy verses will not last these three days, mine will to all time. " Which was as much as to tell him he could not write a verse. I have met many of these rattles that made a noise and buzzed. They had their hum, and

no more. Indeed, things wrote with labour deserve to be so read, and will last their age.

3. Imitatio. —Horatius. —Virgil. —Statius. —Homer. —Horat. — Archil. —Alcaeus, &c. —The third requisite in our poet or maker is imitation, to be able to convert the substance or riches of another poet to his own use. To make choice of one excellent man above the rest, and so to follow him till he grow very he, or so like him as the copy may be mistaken for the principal. Not as a creature that swallows what it takes in crude, raw, or undigested, but that feeds with an appetite, and hath a stomach to concoct, divide, and turn all into nourishment. Not to imitate servilely, as Horace saith, and catch at vices for virtue, but to draw forth out of the best and choicest flowers, with the bee, and turn all into honey, work it into one relish and savour; make our imitation sweet; observe how the best writers have imitated, and follow them. How Virgil and Statius have imitated Homer; how Horace, Archilochus; how Alcaeus, and the other lyrics; and so of the rest.

4. Lectio. —Parnassus. —Helicon. —Arscoron. —M. T. Cicero. — Simylus. —Stob. —Horat. —Aristot. —But that which we especially require in him is an exactness of study and multiplicity of reading, which maketh a full man, not alone enabling him to know the history or argument of a poem and to report it, but so to master the matter and style, as to show he knows how to handle, place, or dispose of either with elegancy when need shall be. And not think he can leap forth suddenly a poet by dreaming he hath been in Parnassus, or having washed his lips, as they say, in Helicon. There goes more to his making than so; for to nature, exercise, imitation, and study art must be added to make all these perfect. And though these challenge to themselves much in the making up of our maker, it is Art only can lead him to perfection, and leave him there in possession, as planted by her hand. It is the assertion of Tully, if to an excellent nature there happen an accession or conformation of learning and discipline, there will then remain somewhat noble and singular. For, as Simylus saith in Stobaeus, [Greek text], without art nature can never be perfect; and without nature art can claim no being. But our poet must beware that his study be not only to learn of himself; for he that shall affect to do that confesseth his ever having a fool to his master. He must read many, but ever the best and choicest; those that can teach him anything he must ever account his masters, and reverence. Among whom Horace and (he that taught him) Aristotle deserved to be the first in estimation. Aristotle

was the first accurate critic and truest judge—nay, the greatest philosopher the world ever had—for he noted the vices of all knowledges in all creatures, and out of many men's perfections in a science he formed still one art. So he taught us two offices together, how we ought to judge rightly of others, and what we ought to imitate specially in ourselves. But all this in vain without a natural wit and a poetical nature in chief. For no man, so soon as he knows this or reads it, shall be able to write the better; but as he is adapted to it by nature, he shall grow the perfecter writer. He must have civil prudence and eloquence, and that whole; not taken up by snatches or pieces in sentences or remnants when he will handle business or carry counsels, as if he came then out of the declaimer's gallery, or shadow furnished but out of the body of the State, which commonly is the school of men.

Virorum schola respub. —Lysippus. —Apelles. —Naevius. —The poet is the nearest borderer upon the orator, and expresseth all his virtues, though he be tied more to numbers, is his equal in ornament, and above him in his strengths. And (of the kind) the comic comes nearest; because in moving the minds of men, and stirring of affections (in which oratory shows, and especially approves her eminence), he chiefly excels. What figure of a body was Lysippus ever able to form with his graver, or Apelles to paint with his pencil, as the comedy to life expresseth so many and various affections of the mind? There shall the spectator see some insulting with joy, others fretting with melancholy, raging with anger, mad with love, boiling with avarice, undone with riot, tortured with expectation, consumed with fear; no perturbation in common life but the orator finds an example of it in the scene. And then for the elegancy of language, read but this inscription on the grave of a comic poet:

> "Immortales mortales si fas esset fiere,
> Flerent divae Camoenae Naevium poetam;
> Itaque postquam est Orcino traditus thesauro,
> Obliti sunt Romae lingua loqui Latina. " {146a}

L. AElius Stilo. —Plautus. —M. Varro. —Or that modester testimony given by Lucius AElius Stilo upon Plautus, who affirmed, "Musas, si Latine loqui voluissent, Plautino sermone fuisse loquuturas. " And that illustrious judgment by the most learned M. Varro of him, who pronounced him the prince of letters and elegancy in the Roman language.

Sophocles. —I am not of that opinion to conclude a poet's liberty within the narrow limits of laws which either the grammarians or philosophers prescribe. For before they found out those laws there were many excellent poets that fulfilled them, amongst whom none more perfect than Sophocles, who lived a little before Aristotle.

Demosthenes. —Pericles. —Alcibiades. —Which of the Greeklings durst ever give precepts to Demosthenes? or to Pericles, whom the age surnamed Heavenly, because he seemed to thunder and lighten with his language? or to Alcibiades, who had rather Nature for his guide than Art for his master?

Aristotle. —But whatsoever nature at any time dictated to the most happy, or long exercise to the most laborious, that the wisdom and learning of Aristotle hath brought into an art, because he understood the causes of things; and what other men did by chance or custom he doth by reason; and not only found out the way not to err, but the short way we should take not to err.

Euripides. —Aristophanes. —Many things in Euripides hath Aristophanes wittily reprehended, not out of art, but out of truth. For Euripides is sometimes peccant, as he is most times perfect. But judgment when it is greatest, if reason doth not accompany it, is not ever absolute.

Cens. Scal. in Lil. Germ. —Horace. —To judge of poets is only the faculty of poets; and not of all poets, but the best. Nemo infelicius de poetis judicavit, quam qui de poetis scripsit. {148a} But some will say critics are a kind of tinkers, that make more faults than they mend ordinarily. See their diseases and those of grammarians. It is true, many bodies are the worse for the meddling with; and the multitude of physicians hath destroyed many sound patients with their wrong practice. But the office of a true critic or censor is, not to throw by a letter anywhere, or damn an innocent syllable, but lay the words together, and amend them; judge sincerely of the author and his matter, which is the sign of solid and perfect learning in a man. Such was Horace, an author of much civility, and (if any one among the heathen can be) the best master both of virtue and wisdom; an excellent and true judge upon cause and reason, not because he thought so, but because he knew so out of use and experience.
Cato, the grammarian, a defender of Lucilius. {149a}

"Cato grammaticus, Latina syren,

Qui solus legit, et facit poetas. "

Quintilian of the same heresy, but rejected. {149b}

Horace, his judgment of Choerillus defended against Joseph Scaliger. {149c} And of Laberius against Julius. {149d}

But chiefly his opinion of Plautus {149e} vindicated against many that are offended, and say it is a hard censure upon the parent of all conceit and sharpness. And they wish it had not fallen from so great a master and censor in the art, whose bondmen knew better how to judge of Plautus than any that dare patronise the family of learning in this age; who could not be ignorant of the judgment of the times in which he lived, when poetry and the Latin language were at the height; especially being a man so conversant and inwardly familiar with the censures of great men that did discourse of these things daily amongst themselves. Again, a man so gracious and in high favour with the Emperor, as Augustus often called him his witty manling (for the littleness of his stature), and, if we may trust antiquity, had designed him for a secretary of estate, and invited him to the palace, which he modestly prayed off and refused.

Terence. —Menander. Horace did so highly esteem Terence's comedies, as he ascribes the art in comedy to him alone among the Latins, and joins him with Menander.

Now, let us see what may be said for either, to defend Horace's judgment to posterity and not wholly to condemn Plautus.

The parts of a comedy and tragedy. —The parts of a comedy are the same with a tragedy, and the end is partly the same, for they both delight and teach; the comics are called [Greek text], of the Greeks no less than the tragics.

Aristotle. —Plato. —Homer. —Nor is the moving of laughter always the end of comedy; that is rather a fowling for the people's delight, or their fooling. For, as Aristotle says rightly, the moving of laughter is a fault in comedy, a kind of turpitude that depraves some part of a man's nature without a disease. As a wry face without pain moves laughter, or a deformed vizard, or a rude clown dressed in a lady's habit and using her actions; we dislike and scorn such representations which made the ancient philosophers ever think laughter unfitting in a wise man. And this induced Plato to esteem of

Homer as a sacrilegious person, because he presented the gods sometimes laughing. As also it is divinely said of Aristotle, that to seen ridiculous is a part of dishonesty, and foolish.

The wit of the old comedy. —So that what either in the words or sense of an author, or in the language or actions of men, is awry or depraved does strangely stir mean affections, and provoke for the most part to laughter. And therefore it was clear that all insolent and obscene speeches, jests upon the best men, injuries to particular persons, perverse and sinister sayings (and the rather unexpected) in the old comedy did move laughter, especially where it did imitate any dishonesty, and scurrility came forth in the place of wit, which, who understands the nature and genius of laughter cannot but perfectly know.

Aristophanes. —Plautus. —Of which Aristophanes affords an ample harvest, having not only outgone Plautus or any other in that kind, but expressed all the moods and figures of what is ridiculous oddly. In short, as vinegar is not accounted good until the wine be corrupted, so jests that are true and natural seldom raise laughter with the beast the multitude. They love nothing that is right and proper. The farther it runs from reason or possibility with them the better it is.

Socrates. —Theatrical wit. —What could have made them laugh, like to see Socrates presented, that example of all good life, honesty, and virtue, to have him hoisted up with a pulley, and there play the philosopher in a basket; measure how many foot a flea could skip geometrically, by a just scale, and edify the people from the engine. This was theatrical wit, right stage jesting, and relishing a playhouse, invented for scorn and laughter; whereas, if it had savoured of equity, truth, perspicuity, and candour, to have tasten a wise or a learned palate, —spit it out presently! this is bitter and profitable: this instructs and would inform us: what need we know any thing, that are nobly born, more than a horse-race, or a hunting-match, our day to break with citizens, and such innate mysteries?

The cart. —This is truly leaping from the stage to the tumbril again, reducing all wit to the original dung-cart.

Of the magnitude and compass of any fable, epic or dramatic.

What the measure of a fable is. — The fable or plot of a poem defined. — The epic fable, differing from the dramatic. — To the resolving of this question we must first agree in the definition of the fable. The fable is called the imitation of one entire and perfect action, whose parts are so joined and knit together, as nothing in the structure can be changed, or taken away, without impairing or troubling the whole, of which there is a proportionable magnitude in the members. As for example: if a man would build a house, he would first appoint a place to build it in, which he would define within certain bounds; so in the constitution of a poem, the action is aimed at by the poet, which answers place in a building, and that action hath his largeness, compass, and proportion. But as a court or king's palace requires other dimensions than a private house, so the epic asks a magnitude from other poems, since what is place in the one is action in the other; the difference is an space. So that by this definition we conclude the fable to be the imitation of one perfect and entire action, as one perfect and entire place is required to a building. By perfect, we understand that to which nothing is wanting, as place to the building that is raised, and action to the fable that is formed. It is perfect, perhaps not for a court or king's palace, which requires a greater ground, but for the structure he would raise; so the space of the action may not prove large enough for the epic fable, yet be perfect for the dramatic, and whole.

What we understand by whole. — Whole we call that, and perfect, which hath a beginning, a midst, and an end. So the place of any building may be whole and entire for that work, though too little for a palace. As to a tragedy or a comedy, the action may be convenient and perfect that would not fit an epic poem in magnitude. So a lion is a perfect creature in himself, though it be less than that of a buffalo or a rhinocerote. They differ but in specie: either in the kind is absolute; both have their parts, and either the whole. Therefore, as in every body so in every action, which is the subject of a just work, there is required a certain proportionable greatness, neither too vast nor too minute. For that which happens to the eyes when we behold a body, the same happens to the memory when we contemplate an action. I look upon a monstrous giant, as Tityus, whose body covered nine acres of land, and mine eye sticks upon every part; the whole that consists of those parts will never be taken in at one entire view. So in a fable, if the action be too great, we can never comprehend the whole together in our imagination. Again, if it be too little, there ariseth no pleasure out of the object; it affords the view no stay; it is beheld, and vanisheth at once. As if we should look upon an ant or pismire, the parts fly the sight, and the whole considered is almost nothing. The same happens in action, which is the object of memory, as the body is of sight. Too vast oppresseth the eyes, and exceeds the memory; too little scarce admits either.

What is the utmost bounds of a fable. —Now in every action it behoves the poet to know which is his utmost bound, how far with fitness and a necessary proportion he may produce and determine it; that is, till either good fortune change into the worse, or the worse into the better. For as a body without proportion cannot be goodly, no more can the action, either in comedy or tragedy, without his fit bounds: and every bound, for the nature of the subject, is esteemed the best that is largest, till it can increase no more; so it behoves the action in tragedy or comedy to be let grow till the necessity ask a conclusion; wherein two things are to be considered: first, that it exceed not the compass of one day; next, that there be place left for digression and art. For the episodes and digressions in a fable are the same that household stuff and other furniture are in a house. And so far from the measure and extent of a fable dramatic.

What by one and entire. —Now that it should be one and entire. One is considerable two ways; either as it is only separate, and by itself, or as being composed of many parts, it begins to be one as those parts grow or are wrought together. That it should be one the first away alone, and by itself, no man that hath tasted letters ever would say, especially having required before a just magnitude and equal proportion of the parts in themselves. Neither of which can possibly be, if the action be single and separate, not composed of parts, which laid together in themselves, with an equal and fitting proportion, tend to the same end; which thing out of antiquity itself hath deceived many, and more this day it doth deceive.

Hercules. —Theseus. —Achilles. —Ulysses. —Homer and Virgil. — AEneas. —Venus. —So many there be of old that have thought the action of one man to be one, as of Hercules, Theseus, Achilles, Ulysses, and other heroes; which is both foolish and false, since by one and the same person many things may be severally done which cannot fitly be referred or joined to the same end: which not only the excellent tragic poets, but the best masters of the epic, Homer and Virgil, saw. For though the argument of an epic poem be far more diffused and poured out than that of tragedy, yet Virgil, writing of AEneas, hath pretermitted many things. He neither tells how he was born, how brought up, how he fought with Achilles, how he was snatched out of the battle by Venus; but that one thing, how he came into Italy, he prosecutes in twelve books. The rest of his journey, his error by sea, the sack of Troy, are put not as the argument of the work, but episodes of the argument. So Homer laid by many things of Ulysses, and handled no more than he saw tended to one and the same end.

Theseus. —Hercules. —Juvenal. —Codrus. —Sophocles. —Ajax. — Ulysses. - -Contrary to which, and foolishly, those poets did, whom the philosopher taxeth, of whom one gathered all the actions of Theseus, another put all the labours of Hercules in one work. So did he whom Juvenal mentions in the beginning, "hoarse Codrus, " that recited a volume compiled, which he called his Theseide, not yet finished, to the great trouble both of his hearers and himself; amongst which there were many parts had no coherence nor kindred one with another, so far they were from being one action, one fable. For as a house, consisting of divers materials, becomes one structure and one dwelling, so an action, composed of divers parts, may become one fable, epic or dramatic. For example, in a tragedy, look upon Sophocles, his Ajax: Ajax, deprived of Achilles' armour, which he hoped from the suffrage of the Greeks, disdains; and, growing impatient of the injury, rageth, and runs mad. In that humour he doth many senseless things, and at last falls upon the Grecian flock and kills a great ram for Ulysses: returning to his senses, he grows ashamed of the scorn, and kills himself; and is by the chiefs of the Greeks forbidden burial. These things agree and hang together, not as they were done, but as seeming to be done, which made the action whole, entire, and absolute.

The conclusion concerning the whole, and the parts. —Which are episodes. —Ajax and Hector. —Homer. —For the whole, as it consisteth of parts, so without all the parts it is not the whole; and to make it absolute is required not only the parts, but such parts as are true. For a part of the whole was true; which, if you take away, you either change the whole or it is not the whole. For if it be such a part, as, being present or absent, nothing concerns the whole, it cannot be called a part of the whole; and such are the episodes, of which hereafter. For the present here is one example: the single combat of Ajax with Hector, as it is at large described in Homer, nothing belongs to this Ajax of Sophocles.

You admire no poems but such as run like a brewer's cart upon the stones, hobbling: -

"Et, quae per salebras, altaque saxa cadunt,
    Accius et quidquid Pacuviusque vomunt.
Attonitusque legis terrai, frugiferai. " {160a}

SOME POEMS.

TO WILLIAM CAMDEN

Camden! most reverend head, to whom I owe
All that I am in arts, all that I know –
How nothing's that! to whom my country owes
The great renown, and name wherewith she goes!
Than thee the age sees not that thing more grave,
More high, more holy, that she more would crave.
What name, what skill, what faith hast thou in things!
What sight in searching the most antique springs!
What weight, and what authority in thy speech!
Men scarce can make that doubt, but thou canst teach.
Pardon free truth, and let thy modesty,
Which conquers all, be once o'ercome by thee.
Many of thine, this better could, than I;
But for their powers, accept my piety.

ON MY FIRST DAUGHTER

Here lies, to each her parents' ruth,
Mary, the daughter of their youth;
Yet, all heaven's gifts, being heaven's due,
It makes the father less to rue.
At six months' end, she parted hence,
With safety of her innocence;
Whose soul heaven's queen, whose name she bears,
In comfort of her mother's tears,
Hath placed amongst her virgin-train;
Where, while that severed doth remain,
This grave partakes the fleshly birth;
Which cover lightly, gentle earth!

ON MY FIRST SON

Farewell, thou child of my right hand, and joy;
My sin was too much hope of thee, loved boy;
Seven years thou wert lent to me, and I thee pay,
Exacted by thy fate, on the just day.
Oh! could I lose all father, now! for why,
Will man lament the state he should envy?

To have so soon 'scaped world's, and flesh's rage,
And, if no other misery, yet age!
Rest in soft peace, and, asked, say here doth lie
Ben Jonson his best piece of poetry;
For whose sake, henceforth, all his vows be such,
As what he loves may never like too much.

TO FRANCIS BEAUMONT

How I do love thee, Beaumont, and thy muse,
That unto me dost such religion use!
How I do fear myself, that am not worth
The least indulgent thought thy pen drops forth!
At once thou mak'st me happy, and unmak'st;
And giving largely to me, more thou takest!
What fate is mine, that so itself bereaves?
What art is thine, that so thy friend deceives?
When even there, where most thou praisest me,
For writing better, I must envy thee.

OF LIFE AND DEATH

The ports of death are sins; of life, good deeds:
Through which our merit leads us to our meeds.
How wilful blind is he, then, that would stray,
And hath it in his powers to make his way!
This world death's region is, the other life's:
And here it should be one of our first strifes,
So to front death, as men might judge us past it:
For good men but see death, the wicked taste it.

INVITING A FRIEND TO SUPPER

To-night, grave sir, both my poor house and I
Do equally desire your company;
Not that we think us worthy such a guest,
But that your worth will dignify our feast,
With those that come; whose grace may make that seem
Something, which else could hope for no esteem.
It is the fair acceptance, sir, creates
The entertainment perfect, not the cates.
Yet shall you have, to rectify your palate,

An olive, capers, or some bitter salad
Ushering the mutton; with a short-legged hen,
If we can get her, full of eggs, and then,
Lemons and wine for sauce: to these, a coney
Is not to be despaired of for our money;
And though fowl now be scarce, yet there are clerks,
The sky not falling, think we may have larks.
I'll tell you of more, and lie, so you will come:
Of partridge, pheasant, woodcock, of which some
May yet be there; and godwit if we can;
Knat, rail, and ruff, too. Howsoe'er, my man
Shall read a piece of Virgil, Tacitus,
Livy, or of some better book to us,
Of which we'll speak our minds, amidst our meat;
And I'll profess no verses to repeat:
To this if aught appear, which I not know of,
That will the pastry, not my paper, show of.
Digestive cheese, and fruit there sure will be;
But that which most doth take my muse and me,
Is a pure cup of rich canary wine,
Which is the Mermaid's now, but shall be mine:
Of which had Horace, or Anacreon tasted,
Their lives, as do their lines, till now had lasted.
Tobacco, nectar, or the Thespian spring,
Are all but Luther's beer, to this I sing.
Of this we will sup free, but moderately,
And we will have no Pooly' or Parrot by;
Nor shall our cups make any guilty men;
But at our parting we will be as when
We innocently met. No simple word
That shall be uttered at our mirthful board,
Shall make us sad next morning; or affright
The liberty that we'll enjoy to-night.

EPITAPH ON SALATHIEL PAVY, A CHILD OF QUEEN ELIZABETH'S CHAPEL

Weep with me all you that read
  This little story;
And know for whom a tear you shed,
  Death's self is sorry.
'Twas a child that so did thrive
  In grace and feature,

As heaven and nature seemed to strive
  Which owned the creature.
Years he numbered scarce thirteen
  When fates turned cruel;
Yet three filled zodiacs had he been
  The stage's jewel;
And did act, what now we moan,
  Old men so duly;
As, sooth, the Parcae thought him one
  He played so truly.
So, by error to his fate
  They all consented;
But viewing him since, alas, too late!
  They have repented;
And have sought to give new birth,
  In baths to steep him;
But, being so much too good for earth,
  Heaven vows to keep him.

EPITAPH ON ELIZABETH, L. H.

Wouldst thou hear what man can say
In a little? Reader, stay.
Underneath this stone doth lie
As much beauty as could die
Which in life did harbour give
To more virtue than doth live.
If, at all, she had a fault
Leave it buried in this vault.
One name was Elizabeth,
The other let it sleep with death.
Fitter, where it died, to tell,
Than that it lived at all. Farewell.

EPITAPH ON THE COUNTESS OF PEMBROKE

Underneath this sable hearse
Lies the subject of all verse,
Sidney's sister, Pembroke's mother:
Death! ere thou hast slain another,
Learned, and fair, and good as she,
Time shall throw a dart at thee.

TO THE MEMORY OF MY BELOVED MASTER WILLIAM SHAKSPEARE, AND WHAT HE HATH LEFT US

To draw no envy, Shakspeare, on thy name,
Am I thus ample to thy book and fame;
While I confess thy writings to be such,
As neither man, nor muse can praise too much.
'Tis true, and all men's suffrage. But these ways
Were not the paths I meant unto thy praise;
For silliest ignorance on these may light,
Which, when it sounds at best, but echoes right;
Or blind affection, which doth ne'er advance
The truth, but gropes, and urgeth all by chance;
Or crafty malice might pretend this praise,
And think to ruin, where it seemed to raise.
These are, as some infamous bawd, or whore,
Should praise a matron; what would hurt her more?
But thou art proof against them, and, indeed,
Above the ill-fortune of them, or the need.
I, therefore, will begin: Soul of the age!
The applause! delight! and wonder of our stage!
My Shakspeare rise! I will not lodge thee by
Chaucer, or Spenser, or bid Beaumont lie
A little further off, to make thee room:
Thou art a monument without a tomb,
And art alive still, while thy book doth live
And we have wits to read, and praise to give.
That I not mix thee so, my brain excuses,
I mean with great, but disproportioned Muses;
For if I thought my judgment were of years,
I should commit thee surely with thy peers,
And tell how far thou didst our Lily outshine,
Or sporting Kyd, or Marlow's mighty line.
And though thou hadst small Latin and less Greek,
From thence to honour thee, I will not seek
For names: but call forth thundering Eschylus,
Euripides, and Sophocles to us,
Pacuvius, Accius, him of Cordoua dead,
To live again, to hear thy buskin tread,
And shake a stage; or, when thy socks were on,
Leave thee alone for the comparison
Of all that insolent Greece, or haughty Rome
Sent forth, or since did from their ashes come.

Triumph, my Britain, thou hast one to show,
To whom all scenes of Europe homage owe.
He was not of an age, but for all time!
And all the Muses still were in their prime,
When, like Apollo, he came forth to warm
Our ears, or like a Mercury to charm!
Nature herself was proud of his designs,
And joyed to wear the dressing of his lines!
Which were so richly spun, and woven so fit,
As, since, she will vouchsafe no other wit.
The merry Greek, tart Aristophanes,
Neat Terence, witty Plautus, now not please;
But antiquated and deserted lie,
As they were not of nature's family.
Yet must I not give nature all; thy art,
My gentle Shakspeare, must enjoy a part.
For though the poet's matter nature be,
His heart doth give the fashion: and, that he
Who casts to write a living line, must sweat,
(Such as thine are) and strike the second heat
Upon the Muse's anvil; turn the same,
And himself with it, that he thinks to frame;
Or for the laurel, he may gain a scorn;
For a good poet's made, as well as born.
And such wert thou! Look how the father's face
Lives in his issue, even so the race
Of Shakspeare's mind and manners brightly shines
In his well-turned, and true filed lines;
In each of which he seems to shake a lance,
As brandished at the eyes of ignorance.
Sweet Swan of Avon! what a sight it were
To see thee in our water yet appear,
And make those flights upon the banks of Thames,
That so did take Eliza, and our James!
But stay, I see thee in the hemisphere
Advanced, and made a constellation there!
Shine forth, thou star of poets, and with rage,
Or influence, chide, or cheer the drooping stage,
Which, since thy flight from hence, hath mourned like night,
And despairs day, but for thy volume's light.

TO CELIA

Drink to me only with thine eyes,
  And I will pledge with mine;
Or leave a kiss but in the cup,
  And I'll not look for wine.
The thirst that from the soul doth rise
  Doth ask a drink divine:
But might I of Jove's nectar sup,
  I would not change for thine.

I sent thee late a rosy wreath,
  Not so much honouring thee,
As giving it a hope that there
  It could not withered be.
But thou thereon didst only breathe,
  And sent'st it back to me:
Since when it grows, and smells, I swear,
  Not of itself, but thee.

THE TRIUMPH OF CHARIS

See the chariot at hand here of Love,
  Wherein my lady rideth!
Each that draws is a swan or a dove,
  And well the car Love guideth.
As she goes, all hearts do duty
    Unto her beauty;
  And, enamoured, do wish, so they might
    But enjoy such a sight,
That they still were to run by her side,
Through swords, through seas, whither she would ride.

Do but look on her eyes, they do light
  All that Love's world compriseth!
Do but look on her hair, it is bright
  As Love's star when it riseth!
Do but mark, her forehead's smoother
    Than words that soothe her!
And from her arched brows, such a grace
    Sheds itself through the face,
As alone there triumphs to the life
All the gain, all the good, of the elements' strife.

Have you seen but a bright lily grow
  Before rude hands have touched it?
Have you marked but the fall o' the snow
  Before the soil hath smutched it?
Have you felt the wool of beaver?
    Or swan's down ever?
Or have smelt o' the bud o' the brier?
    Or the nard in the fire?
Or have tasted the bag of the bee?
O so white! O so soft! O so sweet is she!

IN THE PERSON OF WOMANKIND
A SONG APOLOGETIC

Men, if you love us, play no more
  The fools or tyrants with your friends,
To make us still sing o'er and o'er
  Our own false praises, for your ends:
    We have both wits and fancies too,
    And, if we must, let's sing of you.

Nor do we doubt but that we can,
  If we would search with care and pain,
Find some one good in some one man;
  So going thorough all your strain,
    We shall, at last, of parcels make
    One good enough for a song's sake.

And as a cunning painter takes,
  In any curious piece you see,
More pleasure while the thing he makes,
  Than when 'tis made--why so will we.
    And having pleased our art, we'll try
    To make a new, and hang that by.

ODE

To the Immortal Memory and Friendship of that Noble Pair, Sir
Lucius Cary and Sir Henry Morison.

I.

THE TURN.

Brave infant of Saguntum, clear
  Thy coming forth in that great year,
When the prodigious Hannibal did crown
His cage, with razing your immortal town.
    Thou, looking then about,
    Ere thou wert half got out,
  Wise child, didst hastily return,
  And mad'st thy mother's womb thine urn.
How summed a circle didst thou leave mankind
Of deepest lore, could we the centre find!

THE COUNTER-TURN.

Did wiser nature draw thee back,
  From out the horror of that sack,
Where shame, faith, honour, and regard of right,
Lay trampled on? the deeds of death and night,
    Urged, hurried forth, and hurled
    Upon th' affrighted world;
  Sword, fire, and famine, with fell fury met,
  And all on utmost ruin set;
As, could they but life's miseries foresee,
No doubt all infants would return like thee.

THE STAND.

For what is life, if measured by the space
    Not by the act?
Or masked man, if valued by his face,
    Above his fact?
  Here's one outlived his peers,
  And told forth fourscore years;
  He vexed time, and busied the whole state;
    Troubled both foes and friends;
    But ever to no ends:
  What did this stirrer but die late?
How well at twenty had he fallen or stood!
For three of his fourscore he did no good.

II.

THE TURN

He entered well, by virtuous parts,
  Got up, and thrived with honest arts;
He purchased friends, and fame, and honours then,
And had his noble name advanced with men:
    But weary of that flight,
    He stooped in all men's sight
      To sordid flatteries, acts of strife,
      And sunk in that dead sea of life,
So deep, as he did then death's waters sup,
But that the cork of title buoyed him up.

THE COUNTER-TURN

Alas! but Morison fell young:
  He never fell,--thou fall'st, my tongue.
He stood a soldier to the last right end,
A perfect patriot, and a noble friend;
    But most, a virtuous son.
    All offices were done
  By him, so ample, full, and round,
  In weight, in measure, number, sound,
As, though his age imperfect might appear,
His life was of humanity the sphere.

THE STAND

Go now, and tell out days summed up with fears,
    And make them years;
Produce thy mass of miseries on the stage,
    To swell thine age;
  Repeat of things a throng,
  To show thou hast been long,
Not lived: for life doth her great actions spell.
  By what was done and wrought
  In season, and so brought
To light: her measures are, how well
Each syllabe answered, and was formed, how fair;
These make the lines of life, and that's her air!

III.

THE TURN

It is not growing like a tree
In bulk, doth make men better be;
Or standing long an oak, three hundred year,
To fall a log at last, dry, bald, and sear:
    A lily of a day,
    Is fairer far in May,
  Although it fall and die that night;
  It was the plant, and flower of light.
In small proportions we just beauties see;
And in short measures, life may perfect be.

THE COUNTER-TURN

Call, noble Lucius, then for wine,
  And let thy looks with gladness shine:
Accept this garland, plant it on thy head
And think, nay know, thy Morison's not dead
    He leaped the present age,
    Possessed with holy rage
  To see that bright eternal day;
  Of which we priests and poets say,
Such truths, as we expect for happy men:
And there he lives with memory and Ben.

THE STAND

Jonson, who sung this of him, ere he went,
    Himself to rest,
Or taste a part of that full joy he meant
    To have expressed,
   In this bright Asterism!
   Where it were friendship's schism,
  Were not his Lucius long with us to tarry,
   To separate these twi-
   Lights, the Dioscouri;
  And keep the one half from his Harry,
But fate doth so alternate the design
Whilst that in heaven, this light on earth must shine.

IV.

THE TURN

And shine as you exalted are;
  Two names of friendship, but one star:
Of hearts the union, and those not by chance
Made, or indenture, or leased out t'advance
    The profits for a time.
    No pleasures vain did chime,
  Of rhymes, or riots, at your feasts,
  Orgies of drink, or feigned protests:
But simple love of greatness and of good,
That knits brave minds and manners more than blood.

THE COUNTER-TURN

This made you first to know the why
  You liked, then after, to apply
That liking; and approach so one the t'other,
Till either grew a portion of the other:
    Each styled by his end,
    The copy of his friend.
  You lived to be the great sir-names,
  And titles, by which all made claims
Unto the virtue; nothing perfect done,
But as a Cary, or a Morison.

THE STAND

And such a force the fair example had,
    As they that saw
The good, and durst not practise it, were glad
    That such a law
  Was left yet to mankind;
  Where they might read and find
  Friendship, indeed, was written not in words;
  And with the heart, not pen,
  Of two so early men,
  Whose lines her rolls were, and records;
Who, ere the first down bloomed upon the chin,
Had sowed these fruits, and got the harvest in.

PRAELUDIUM

And must I sing? What subject shall I choose!
Or whose great name in poets' heaven use,
For the more countenance to my active muse?

Hercules? alas, his bones are yet sore
With his old earthly labours t' exact more
Of his dull godhead were sin. I'll implore

Phoebus. No, tend thy cart still. Envious day
Shall not give out that I have made thee stay,
And foundered thy hot team, to tune my lay.

Nor will I beg of thee, lord of the vine,
To raise my spirits with thy conjuring wine,
In the green circle of thy ivy twine.

Pallas, nor thee I call on, mankind maid,
That at thy birth mad'st the poor smith afraid.
Who with his axe thy father's midwife played.

Go, cramp dull Mars, light Venus, when he snorts,
Or with thy tribade trine invent new sports;
Thou, nor thy looseness with my making sorts.

Let the old boy, your son, ply his old task,
Turn the stale prologue to some painted mask;
His absence in my verse is all I ask.

Hermes, the cheater, shall not mix with us,
Though he would steal his sisters' Pegasus,
And rifle him; or pawn his petasus.

Nor all the ladies of the Thespian lake,
Though they were crushed into one form, could make
A beauty of that merit, that should take

My muse up by commission; no, I bring
My own true fire: now my thought takes wing,
And now an epode to deep ears I sing.

EPODE

Not to know vice at all, and keep true state,
    Is virtue and not fate:
Next to that virtue, is to know vice well,
    And her black spite expel.
Which to effect (since no breast is so sure,
    Or safe, but she'll procure
Some way of entrance) we must plant a guard
    Of thoughts to watch and ward
At th' eye and ear, the ports unto the mind,
    That no strange, or unkind
Object arrive there, but the heart, our spy,
    Give knowledge instantly
To wakeful reason, our affections' king:
    Who, in th' examining,
Will quickly taste the treason, and commit
    Close, the close cause of it.
'Tis the securest policy we have,
    To make our sense our slave.
But this true course is not embraced by many:
    By many! scarce by any.
For either our affections do rebel,
    Or else the sentinel,
That should ring 'larum to the heart, doth sleep:
    Or some great thought doth keep
Back the intelligence, and falsely swears
    They're base and idle fears
Whereof the loyal conscience so complains.
    Thus, by these subtle trains,
Do several passions invade the mind,
    And strike our reason blind:
Of which usurping rank, some have thought love
    The first: as prone to move
Most frequent tumults, horrors, and unrests,
    In our inflamed breasts:
But this doth from the cloud of error grow,
    Which thus we over-blow.
The thing they here call love is blind desire,
    Armed with bow, shafts, and fire;
Inconstant, like the sea, of whence 'tis born,
    Rough, swelling, like a storm;
With whom who sails, rides on the surge of fear,

And boils as if he were
In a continual tempest. Now, true love
  No such effects doth prove;
That is an essence far more gentle, fine,
  Pure, perfect, nay, divine;
It is a golden chain let down from heaven,
  Whose links are bright and even;
That falls like sleep on lovers, and combines
  The soft and sweetest minds
In equal knots: this bears no brands, nor darts,
  To murder different hearts,
But, in a calm and god-like unity,
  Preserves community.
O, who is he that, in this peace, enjoys
  Th' elixir of all joys?
A form more fresh than are the Eden bowers,
  And lasting as her flowers;
Richer than Time and, as Times's virtue, rare;
  Sober as saddest care;
A fixed thought, an eye untaught to glance;
  Who, blest with such high chance,
Would, at suggestion of a steep desire,
  Cast himself from the spire
Of all his happiness? But soft: I hear
  Some vicious fool draw near,
That cries, we dream, and swears there's no such thing,
  As this chaste love we sing.
Peace, Luxury! thou art like one of those
  Who, being at sea, suppose,
Because they move, the continent doth so:
  No, Vice, we let thee know
Though thy wild thoughts with sparrows' wings do fly,
  Turtles can chastely die;
And yet (in this t' express ourselves more clear)
  We do not number here
Such spirits as are only continent,
  Because lust's means are spent;
Or those who doubt the common mouth of fame,
  And for their place and name,
Cannot so safely sin: their chastity
  Is mere necessity;
Nor mean we those whom vows and conscience
  Have filled with abstinence:

Though we acknowledge who can so abstain,
  Makes a most blessed gain;
He that for love of goodness hateth ill,
  Is more crown-worthy still
Than he, which for sin's penalty forbears:
  His heart sins, though he fears.
But we propose a person like our Dove,
  Graced with a Phoenix' love;
A beauty of that clear and sparkling light,
  Would make a day of night,
And turn the blackest sorrows to bright joys:
  Whose odorous breath destroys
All taste of bitterness, and makes the air
  As sweet as she is fair.
A body so harmoniously composed,
  As if nature disclosed
All her best symmetry in that one feature!
  O, so divine a creature
Who could be false to? chiefly, when he knows
  How only she bestows
The wealthy treasure of her love on him;
  Making his fortunes swim
In the full flood of her admired perfection?
  What savage, brute affection,
Would not be fearful to offend a dame
  Of this excelling frame?
Much more a noble, and right generous mind,
  To virtuous moods inclined,
That knows the weight of guilt: he will refrain
  From thoughts of such a strain,
And to his sense object this sentence ever,
  "Man may securely sin, but safely never."

AN ELEGY

Though beauty be the mark of praise,
  And yours, of whom I sing, be such
  As not the world can praise too much,
Yet is 't your virtue now I raise.

A virtue, like allay, so gone
  Throughout your form, as though that move,
  And draw, and conquer all men's love,

This subjects you to love of one,

Wherein you triumph yet: because
   'Tis of yourself, and that you use
   The noblest freedom, not to choose
Against or faith, or honour's laws.

But who could less expect from you,
   In whom alone Love lives again?
   By whom he is restored to men;
And kept, and bred, and brought up true?

His falling temples you have reared,
   The withered garlands ta'en away;
   His altars kept from the decay
That envy wished, and nature feared;

And on them burns so chaste a flame,
   With so much loyalty's expense,
   As Love, t' acquit such excellence,
Is gone himself into your name.

And you are he: the deity
   To whom all lovers are designed,
   That would their better objects find;
Among which faithful troop am I;

Who, as an offering at your shrine,
   Have sung this hymn, and here entreat
   One spark of your diviner heat
To light upon a love of mine;

Which, if it kindle not, but scant
   Appear, and that to shortest view,
   Yet give me leave t' adore in you
What I, in her, am grieved to want.

FOOTNOTES:

{11} "So live with yourself that you do not know how ill yow mind is furnished. "

{12} [Greek text]

{14} "A Puritan is a Heretical Hypocrite, in whom the conceit of his own perspicacity, by which he seems to himself to have observed certain errors in a few Church dogmas, has disturbed the balance of his mind, so that, excited vehemently by a sacred fury, he fights frenzied against civil authority, in the belief that he so pays obedience to God. "

{17a} Night gives counsel.

{17b} Plutarch in Life of Alexander. "Let it not be, O King, that you know these things better than I. "

{19a} "They were not our lords, but our leaders. "

{19b} "Much of it is left also for those who shall be hereafter. "

{19c} "No art is discovered at once and absolutely. "

{22} With a great belly. Comes de Schortenhien.

{23} "In all things I have a better wit and courage than good fortune. "

{24a} "The rich soil exhausts; but labour itself is an aid. "

{24b} "And the gesticulation is vile. "

{25a} "An end is to be looked for in every man, an animal most prompt to change. "

{25b} Arts are not shared among heirs.

{31a} "More loquacious than eloquent; words enough, but little wisdom. " —Sallust.

{31b} Repeated in the following Latin. "The best treasure is in that man's tongue, and he has mighty thanks, who metes out each thing in a few words. " —Hesiod.

{31c} Vid. Zeuxidis pict. Serm. ad Megabizum. —Plutarch.

{32a} "While the unlearned is silent he may be accounted wise, for he has covered by his silence the diseases of his mind. "

{32b} Taciturnity.

{33a} "Hold your tongue above all things, after the example of the gods. " —See Apuleius.

{33b} "Press down the lip with the finger. " —Juvenal.

{33c} Plautus.

{33d} Trinummus, Act 2, Scen. 4.

{34a} "It was the lodging of calamity. " —Mart. lib. 1, ep. 85.

{41} ["Ficta omnia celeriter tanquam flosculi decidunt, nec simulatum potest quidquam esse diuturnum. " —Cicero.]

{44a} Let a Punic sponge go with the book. —Mart. 1. iv. epig. 10.

{47a} He had to be repressed.

{49a} A wit-stand.

{49b} Martial. lib. xi. epig. 91. That fall over the rough ways and high rocks.

{59a} Sir Thomas More. Sir Thomas Wiat. Henry Earl of Surrey. Sir Thomas Chaloner. Sir Thomas Smith. Sir Thomas Eliot. Bishop Gardiner. Sir Nicolas Bacon, L.K. Sir Philip Sidney. Master Richard Hooker. Robert Earl of Essex. Sir Walter Raleigh. Sir Henry Savile. Sir Edwin Sandys. Sir Thomas Egerton, L.C. Sir Francis Bacon, L.C.

{62a} "Which will secure a long age for the known writer. " —Horat. de Art. Poetica.

Discoveries Made Upon Men and Matter and Some Poems

{66a} They have poison for their food, even for their dainty.

{74a} Haud infima ars in principe, ubi lenitas, ubi severitas—plus polleat in commune bonum callere.

{74b} i. e., Machiavell.

{81a} "Censure pardons the crows and vexes the doves. "—Juvenal.

{81b} "Does not spread his net for the hawk or the kite. "—Plautus.

{93} Parrhasius. Eupompus. Socrates. Parrhasius. Clito. Polygnotus. Aglaophon. Zeuxis. Parrhasius. Raphael de Urbino. Mich. Angelo Buonarotti. Titian. Antony de Correg. Sebast. de Venet. Julio Romano. Andrea Sartorio.

{94} Plin. lib. 35. c. 2, 5, 6, and 7. Vitruv. lib. 8 and 7.

{95} Horat. in "Arte Poet. "

{106a} Livy, Sallust, Sidney, Donne, Gower, Chaucer, Spenser, Virgil, Ennius, Homer, Quintilian, Plautus, Terence.

{110a} The interpreter of gods and men.

{111a} Julius Caesar. Of words, see Hor. "De Art. Poet. ; " Quintil. 1. 8, "Ludov. Vives, " pp. 6 and 7.

{111b} A prudent man conveys nothing rashly.

{114a} That jolt as they fall over the rough places and the rocks.

{116a} Directness enlightens, obliquity and circumlocution darken.

{117a} Ocean trembles as if indignant that you quit the land.

{117b} You might believe that the uprooted Cyclades were floating in.

{118a} Those armies of the people of Rome that might break through the heavens. —Caesar. Comment. circa fin.

{124a} No one can speak rightly unless he apprehends wisely.

{133a} "Where the discussion of faults is general, no one is injured. "

{133b} "Gnaw tender little ears with biting truth—Per Sat. 1.

{133c} "The wish for remedy is always truer than the hope. —Livius.

{136a} "AEneas dedicates these arms concerning the conquering Greeks. "—Virg. AEn. lib. 3.

{136b} "You buy everything, Castor; the time will come when you will sell everything. "—Martial, lib. 8, epig. 19.

{136c} "Cinna wishes to seem poor, and is poor. "

{136d} "Which is evident in every first song. "

{139a} "There is a god within us, and when he is stirred we grow warm; that spirit comes from heavenly realms. "

{146a} "If it were allowable for immortals to weep for mortals, the Muses would weep for the poet Naevius; since he is handed to the chamber of Orcus, they have forgotten how to speak Latin at Rome.

{148a} "No one has judged poets less happily than he who wrote about them. "—Senec. de Brev. Vit, cap. 13, et epist. 88.

{149a} Heins, de Sat. 265.

{149b} Pag. 267.

{149c} Pag. 270. 271.

{149d} Pag. 273, et seq.

{149e} Pag. in comm. 153, et seq.

{160a} "And which jolt as they fall over the rough uneven road and high rocks. "—Martial, lib. xi. epig. 91.

Lightning Source UK Ltd.
Milton Keynes UK
178649UK00001B/111/A